The Lawyer's Secret

The Lawyer's Secret

M.E. Braddon

ET REMOTISSIMA PROPE

Hesperus Classics

Hesperus Classics
Published by Hesperus Press Limited
4 Rickett Street, London sw6 1ru
www.hesperuspress.com

First published in 1862
First published by Hesperus Press Limited, 2009

Foreword © Matthew Sweet, 2009

Designed and typeset by Fraser Muggeridge studio
Printed in Jordan by Al-Khayyam Printing Press

isbn: 978-1-84391-189-0

CONTENTS

Before the details of his shame are explicitly revealed, you are likely to have divined the nature of the lawyer's secret. Before the sinister green baize door at the end of the gallery is thrown wide open, you will probably have deduced the identity of the person concealed by the mystery at Fernwood. The author of these stories was no Ellery Queen. She didn't write whodunits. If you like a plot to end with a big surprise involving a smartly-dressed recidivist in the billiard room with a candlestick, then you should probably put this book down. If, however, you have ever suspected a loved one of deception, and nursed that suspicion before speaking your mind, then keep reading. Mary Elizabeth Braddon wrote about secrets and lies; about the experience of living in a family haunted by something that cannot easily be discussed, or of living with a partner whose behaviour raises suspicions that, once acknowledged, may bring a marriage crashing down. Her subject was the tightrope walk of domestic life.

Braddon wrote with enviable energy, often working on several stories simultaneously – some for upmarket shilling periodicals printed on shiny paper; some for cheap magazines that used the kind of ink that came off all over your fingers. In 1861, the year in which *The Lawyer's Secret* ran in *St James's Magazine* and *The Mystery at Fernwood* occupied the readers of *Temple Bar*, she also published a book of poems about Giuseppe Garibaldi, the Italian military hero; rewrote her lurid detective serial *Three Times Dead!!!; or, The Secret of the Heath* (1860) as a respectable three-volume novel entitled *The Trail of the Serpent*; bashed out, anonymously, two rambling blood-and-thunder serials for the *Halfpenny Journal*, a slightly scruffy periodical owned by her partner, James

Maxwell; supplied a novel, *The Lady Lisle* to a weekly journal called the *Welcome Guest*; and began publishing, in a short-lived tuppenny title named *Robin Goodfellow* (also owned by Maxwell), the novel upon which her reputation still rests, *Lady Audley's Secret*.

There was a name for the type of narratives that she produced, whether they were consumed in inky serial form or bound within calf-covered three-decker boards. Sensation fiction. A species of writing that, according to one of its most vocal detractors, aimed at 'electrifying the nerves of the reader', and, according to the satirists of *Punch*, was conceived for the purpose of 'Harrowing the Mind, Making the Flesh Creep, Causing the Hair to Stand on End, Giving Shocks to the Nervous System, Destroying Conventional Moralities, and generally Unfitting the Public for the Prosaic Avocations of Life.'

Sensation fiction was easy to parody. Its three founding novels were Wilkie Collins's *The Woman in White* (1860), about the insanely complex machinations of a decayed British aristocrat and a bonbon-guzzling Italian Count; Ellen Wood's *East Lynne* (1861) about an adulterous woman disfigured in a railway crash, who returns to the family home in disguise in order to work in the nursery of her estranged children; and Braddon's own *Lady Audley's Secret* (completed 1862), the story of a murderously ambitious Pre-Raphaelite beauty who secures a fortune by shoving her husband down the garden well. (He survives, crawls out, slips quietly away to the gold fields of Australia, and returns years later to wreak his revenge.) But for all its extremity, this was a form of fiction that was also very difficult to resist – no matter how noisily its detractors sniffed at it from the pages of expensive literary journals. It owed its attractiveness to the fact that the satirists were partly right. It was fiction that jangled the nerves; that made the heart beat faster; that gave a queasy kind of pleasure which readers felt more in their bodies than in their minds. And in this, it was perfectly attuned to the spirit of the years in which it flourished.

The 1860s were the decade of sensation. In 1864, Henry Longueville Mansel, the Dean of St Paul's Cathedral, used an article in the *Edinburgh Review* to attack Braddon's style of writing and to reflect, with some measure of nostalgia, that 'two or three years ago... nobody would have known what was meant by a sensation novel', but that it had since become 'the regular commercial name for a particular product of industry for which there is just now a brisk demand.' It was a commercial name that might be appended to anything. Readers in the 1860s were alerted to the existence of sensation paragraphs, sensation trials, sensation preachers, sensation steamers, sensation scenes and sensation diplomacy – the latter an Imperial Japanese phenomenon involving public execution and hara-kiri. Throughout the summer of 1861, an enterprising outfitter in the Yorkshire town of Beverley offered shoppers the chance to purchase the 'Sensation Glove', which boasted 'a perfect fit; great elasticity and durability; and first-class colours' – and was also useful, presumably, for customers who wanted to kill their husbands without getting blood under their fingernails.

On stages around the country – but particularly those of the 'transpontine' melodrama houses on the south bank of the Thames – managements produced sensation dramas, plays that supplied an intoxicating combination of nail-biting anxiety and mechanical spectacle. The finale of *Girandella; or, The Child of the Zincali* (1860) pitched a pair of duelling gypsy lovers over a cliff. Dion Boucicault's *The Flying Scud*

(1866) recreated the thrills of Derby Day by sending real horses galloping on concealed conveyor belts. Audiences at Boucicault's *The Colleen Bawn* (1860) exclaimed as the heroine, Eily O'Connor, struggled to keep her head above the waters of a subterranean lake simulated by swatches of gauze and the enthusiastic flapping of a twenty-strong army of stage-hands. Queen Victoria went twice, and during December 1861 – the month that *The Mystery at Fernwood* concluded in *Temple Bar* magazine – it would have been possible for a sensation-seeking Londoner to watch an equestrian version of the play at Astley's Amphitheatre, travel to the Gallery of Illustration to hear the Welsh pianist and comedian John Orlando Parry, 'Relate, Musically, the vicissitudes of the Colleen Bawn', catch the real deal at the New Adelphi Theatre and round off the evening by rolling up the carpet and dancing to the Colleen Bawn Galop [sic] and the Colleen Bawn Polka Mazurka. The producers of burlesque exploited the craze by staging their own parodic versions of the form, among them *Esmeralda; or, The Sensation Goat* and *The Colleen, Drawn (from a novel source); or, The Great Sensation Diving Belle* (both 1861, and both successes in their own right).

Above all these – literally, at least – were the performances of a French acrobat who, in the summer of 1861, began a residency at the Crystal Palace, Joseph Paxton's flatpack glass-and-iron cathedral of the industrial revolution, which had been dismantled in Hyde Park and reassembled in the London suburb of Sydenham. In the vast spaces of the Palace, Blondin – who had once crossed a tightrope stretched across the Niagara Falls – walked through the empty air. He crossed the rope in a monkey costume. He crossed it a suit of armour. He crossed it while cooking an omelette on a portable stove. He crossed it pushing a lion in a wheelbarrow. When he crossed it with his five-year-old daughter, Adele, piggy-backing on his shoulders, the authorities stepped in. 'Thousands of us,' noted Charles Dickens, sitting in the crowd below, 'have come to see an acrobat perform a feat of imminent danger [for the sake of] an exquisite and new sensation.' And that sensation, he conceded, depended upon the 'possibility of painful death'. For some of Blondin's imitators, that possibility was fulfilled: Madame Genieve [sic], one of several turns who pursued a career under the moniker 'the Female Blondin', walked a rope in Birmingham while she was eight months pregnant, and slipped and fell to her destruction. Little wonder that such shows generated an overpowering, anxious pleasure in the bodies of their spectators. 'A few of the younger ladies,' observed Dickens, 'clench their eyebrows in an expression of pain, but still they look up.' How could they avert their eyes?

Braddon's readers followed the relentless forward move- ment of her fiction with a similar apprehension, as, line by febrile line, the heroine advanced across some deep domestic chasm: Ellinor Arden in *The Lawyer's Secret*, negotiating a pragmatic marriage made miserable by the insistent secrecy of two men – her husband, who refuses to allow her to spend money that is hers by right; and her guardian, who is tortured by the memory of a moral transgression he cannot bear to explain; Isabel in *The Mystery at Fernwood*, walking the corridors of a Yorkshire mansion that houses a family secret that is destined to erupt from its hiding place with ferocious violence. Henry James, who was one of Braddon's greatest admirers, celebrated her work for its interest in 'the mysteries which are at our own doors... the terrors of the cheerful country house, or the London lodgings.' Braddon detected the sensational possibilities in the ordinary business of human relations; made shivery fiction from lies, love, deception, betrayal, guilt, and other aspects of family life. The protagonists of these stories must traverse her plots with the same kind of nerve exhibited by Eily O'Connor, struggling in the gauzy water, or a Blondin – male or female – making a vertiginous crossing high above the heads of the crowd. We are down in that crowd, looking up at them. All we need to do is keep our eyes fixed on their progress – to see whether they swim or drown; fall, or make it, unharmed, to the safety of the final paragraph.

– Matthew Sweet, 2009

The Lawyer's Secret

1
IN A LAWYER'S OFFICE

'It is the most provoking clause that was ever invented to annul the advantages of a testament,' said the lady.

'It is a condition which must be fulfilled, or you lose the fortune,' replied the gentleman.

Whereupon the gentleman began to drum a martial air with the tips of fingers upon the morocco-covered office table; while the lady beat time with the point of her foot.

The gentleman was out of temper, and the lady was out of temper also. It is sad to have to state such a fact of a lady, for she was very young and very handsome, and, though the angry light in her dark-grey eyes had a certain vixenish beauty, it was a species of beauty rather alarming to a man of nervous temperament.

She was very handsome. Her hair was of the darkest brown, her eyes grey – those large grey eyes, fringed with long black lashes, which are more dangerous than all other eyes ever invented for the perdition of honest men. They looked like deep pools of shining water, bordered by shadowy rushes; they looked like stray stars in a black midnight sky; but they were so beautiful, that like the signal lamp which announces the advent of an express upon the heels of a slow train, they seemed to say, 'Danger!' Her nose was aquiline; her mouth small, clearly cut, and very determined in expression; her complexion brunette, and rather pale. For the rest she was tall, her head set with a haughty grace upon her sloping shoulders, her hands perfect.

The gentleman was ten or fifteen years her senior. He too was eminently handsome; but there was a languid in-difference about his manner, which communicated itself even to his face, and seemed to overshadow the very beauty of that face.

That anyone so gifted by nature as he seemed gifted could be as weary of life as he appeared, was, in itself, so much a mystery, that one learned to look at him as a man whose quiet outward bearing concealed some gloomy secret.

He was dark and pale, with massive features, and thoughtful brown eyes, which rarely looked fully at you from under the heavy eyelids that half shrouded them. The mouth was spiritual in expression, the lips thin; but the face was wanting in one quality, lacking which it lacked the power which is the highest form of manly beauty; and that quality was firmness.

He sat drumming with his slim fingers upon the table, and looking down, with a gloomy shade upon his forehead.

The scene was a lawyer's office in Gray's Inn. There was a third person present, an elderly lady, rather a faded beauty in appearance, and somewhat overdressed. She took no part in the conversation, but sat in an easy chair by the fire, turning over the crisp sheets of *The Times* newspaper, which, every time she moved them, emitted a sharp, crackling sound, unpleasant to the nervous temperaments of the younger lady and the gentleman.

The gentleman was a solicitor, Horace Margrave, the guardian of the young lady, and executor to her uncle's will. Her name was Ellinor Arden, she was the sole heiress and residuary legatee to her uncle, John Arden, in Northamptonshire; and she had this very day come of age. Mr Margrave had been the trusted and valued friend of her father, dead ten years before, and of her uncle, only lately dead; and Ellinor Arden had been brought up to think, that if there were truth, honesty, or friendship upon earth, those three attributes were centred in the person of Horace Margrave, solicitor, of Gray's Inn.

He is today endeavouring to explain and reconcile her to the conditions of her uncle's will, which are rather peculiar.

'In the first place, my dear Ellinor,' he says, still drumming on the table, still looking at his desk, and not at her, 'you had no particular right to expect to be your uncle John Arden of Arden's heiress.'

'I was his nearest relation,' she said.

'Granted, but that was no more reason why you should be dear to him. Your father and he, after the amiable fashion that frequently obtains among brothers in this very Christian country, were almost strangers to each other for the best part of their lives. You your uncle never saw, since your father lived on his wife's small property in the north of Scotland, and you were brought up in that remote region until your said father's death, which took place ten years ago; after your father's death you were sent to Paris, to be there educated under the surveillance of your aunt, and you therefore never made the acquaintance of John Arden of Arden, your father's only brother.'

'My father had such a horror of being misinterpreted; had he sought to make his daughter known to his rich brother, it might have been thought –'

'That he wanted to get his rich brother's money. It might have been thought? My dear girl, it would have been thought! Your father acted with the pride of the Northamptonshire Ardens; he acted like a high-minded English gentleman; and he acted, in the eyes of the world, like a fool. You never, then, expected to inherit your uncle's money?'

'Never. Nor did I ever wish for it. My mother's little fortune would have been enough for me.'

'I wish to heaven you had never had a penny beyond it.'

As Horace Margrave said these few words, the listless expression of his face was disturbed by a spasm of pain.

He so rarely spoke on any subject whatever in a tone of real earnestness, that Ellinor Arden, startled by the change in his manner, looked up at him suddenly and searchingly. But the veil of weariness had fallen over his face once more, and he continued, with his old indifference –

'To the surprise of everyone, your uncle bequeathed to you, and to you alone, his entire fortune, stranger as you were to him. This was an act, not of love for you, but of duty to his dead brother. The person nearest to his heart was unconnected with him by the ties of kindred, and he no doubt considered that it would be an injustice to disinherit his only brother's child in favour of a stranger. This stranger, this protégé of your uncle's, is the son of a lady who once was beloved by him, but who loved another, poorer and humbler than Squire Arden of Arden. She married this poorer suitor, George Dalton, a young surgeon, in a small country town. She married him, and three years after her marriage, she died leaving an only child, a boy. This boy, on the death of his father, which happened when he was only four years old, was adopted by your uncle. He never married but devoted himself to the education of the son of the woman who had rejected him. He did not, however, bring up the boy to look upon himself as his heir. He educated him as a man ought to be educated who has his own path in life. He gave Dalton a university education, and sent him to the bar, where he pleaded his first cause a year before your father's death. He did not leave the young barrister a shilling.'

'But –'

'But he left his entire fortune to you, on condition that you should marry Henry Dalton within a year of your majority.'

'And if I marry anyone else, or refuse to marry this apothecary's son, I lose the fortune?'

'Every farthing of it.'

A sweet smile brightened her face as she rose hurriedly from her chair, and stood before the table at which the lawyer was seated.

'So be it,' she said resolutely. 'I will forfeit the fortune. I have a hundred a year from my poor mother's estate – enough for any woman. I will forfeit the fortune, and –' she paused for a moment, 'marry the man I love.'

It has been said that Horace Margrave had a pale complexion; but as Ellinor Arden said these words, his face changed from its ordinary dark pallor to a deadly ashen hue, and his strongly marked black eyebrows contracted painfully over his half-closed eyes.

She stood with her small gloved hand resting lightly on the table, and her dark lashes downcast upon the faint crimson of her cheeks, so she did not see the change in Horace Margrave's face. She waited a minute or two, to hear what he would say to her determination; and, on his not speaking, she turned from him impatiently, and resumed her seat.

Nothing could have been more indifferent than Mr Margrave's manner, as he looked lazily up at her, and said,

'My poor romantic child! Throw away a fortune of three thousand a year, to say nothing of Arden Hall, and the broad lands thereto appertaining, and marry the man you love! My sweet, poetical Ellinor, may I venture to ask who this fortunate man may be for whom you are prepared to make such a sacrifice?'

It seemed a very simple and straightforward question, emanating as it did from a man of business, many years her senior, her dead father's old friend, and her own guardian and trustee; but Ellinor Arden appeared painfully embarrassed by it. A dark flush spread itself over her face; and her lips trembled faintly as she tried to speak, and failed to utter a word. She was silent for some minutes, during which Horace Margrave played with a penknife, opening and shutting it absently, and not once looking at his beautiful ward. The elderly lady by the fireplace turned the crackling sheets of *The Times* more than once during the short silence, which seemed so long.

Horace Margrave was the first to speak.

'My dear Ellinor, as your guardian, till this very day possessed of full power of the right to control your actions – after today, I trust, still possessed of the right to advise them – I have surely some claim to your confidence. Tell me, then, candidly – as you may tell a middle-aged solicitor like myself – who is this most happy of mankind? Who is it whom you would rather marry than Henry Dalton, your uncle's adopted son?'

For once he looked at her as he spoke, she looking full at him so that their eyes met. A long, earnest, reproachful, sad look was in hers; in his a darkness of gloomy sorrow, beyond all power of description.

His eyelids were the first to fall; he went on playing with the handle of the penknife, and said,

'You are so long in giving me a candid and straightforward answer, my dear girl, that I begin to think this hero is rather a mythic individual, and that your heart is free. Tell me, Ellinor, is it not so? You have met so few people – have passed so much of your life in the utter seclusion of a Parisian convent – and when away from the convent you have been so protected by the Argus-like guardianship of you respected aunt – that I really cannot conceive how you can have lost that dear, generous heart of yours. I suspect that you are only trying to mystify me. Once and for all, then, my dear ward, has anyone been so fortunate as to win your affections?'

He looked at her as he asked this decisive question with a shrinking upward glance under his dark eyelashes – something like the glance of a man who looks up, expecting a blow, and knows that he must shiver and close his eyes when that blow falls.

The crimson flush passed away from her face, and left her deadly pale, as she said, with a firm voice,

'No!'

'No one?'

'No one.'

Horace Margrave sighed a deep sigh of relief, and proceeded in his former tone – the tone of a thorough man of business.

'Very well, then, my dear Ellinor, seeing that you have formed no prior attachment, that it is your uncle's earnest request, nay, solemn prayer, that this marriage should take place; seeing, also, that Henry Dalton is a very good young man –'

'I hate good young men!' she said impatiently. 'Dreadfully perfect beings, with light hair and fresh-coloured cheeks. Men who sing in church, and wear double-soled boots. I detest them.'

'My dear Ellinor! My dear Ellinor! Life is neither a stage play nor a three-volume novel; and rely upon it, the happiness of a wife depends very little on the colour of her husband's hair, or the cut of his coat. If he neglects you, will you be happier, lonely and deserted at home, in remembering the haughty grace of his head, at that very moment, perhaps bending over the green cloth of a club whist table? If he wrings your heart with the tortures of jealousy, will it console you to recall the splendour of his hazel eyes, whose gaze no longer meets your own? No, no, Ellinor; dispossess yourself of the schoolgirl's notion of Byronic heroes, with turn-down collars, and deficient moral region. Marry Henry Dalton. He is so good, honourable, and sensible, that you must learn to esteem him. Out of that esteem will grow affection; and believe me, paradoxical as it may sound, you will love him better in the future from not loving him too much in the present.'

'As you please, my dear guardian,' replied Miss Arden. 'Henry Dalton by all means, then, and the fortune. I should be very sorry not to follow your excellent, sensible, and business-like advice.'

She said this with a simulation of his own indifference; but, in spite of herself, betrayed considerable agitation.

'If we are to dine at six –' interposed the faded lady by the fireplace, who had been looking over the top of her news-paper every three minutes, hopelessly awaiting a break in the conversation.

'We must go home directly,' replied Ellinor. 'You are right, my dear Mrs Morrison. Pray forgive me. Remember the happiness of a life,' – she looked not at Mrs Morrison, but at Mr Margrave, who had risen and stood leaning against the mantelpiece in an attitude expressive of supreme listlessness, – 'the happiness of a life, perhaps, depended on the interview of today. I have made my decision, at the advice of my guardian. A decision which must, no doubt, result in the happiness of everyone concerned. I am quite at your service, Mrs Morrison.'

Horace Margrave laid his hand on the bell by his side.

'Your carriage will be at the entrance to the Inn in three minutes, Ellinor. I will see you to the gate. Believe me, you have acted wisely; how wisely, you may never know.'

He himself conducted them down the broad panelled staircase, and, putting on his hat, led his ward through the quiet Inn to her carriage. She was grave and silent, and he did not speak to her till she was seated with her elderly companion and chaperone in her roomy landau, when he leaned his hand on the carriage door, and said:

'I shall bring Henry Dalton to Hertford Street this evening, to introduce him to his future wife.'

'Pray do so,' she said. 'Adieu!'

'Only till eight o'clock.'

He lifted his hat, and stood watching the carriage as it drove away, then walked slowly back to his chambers, flung himself in a luxurious easy chair, took a cigar from a small Venetian casket standing on a table at his side, lit it, wheeled his chair close to the fire, planted the heels of his boots against the polished steel of the low grate, and prepared for a lazy half-hour before dinner.

As he lit the cigar, he looked gloomily into the blaze at his feet, and said,

'Horace Margrave, if you had only been an honest man.'

2
IN WHICH A SECRET IS REVEALED

The hands of the ormolu[1] clock, in the little drawing room in Hertford Street occupied by Ellinor Arden and her companion, chaperone, and dependant, Mrs Morrison, pointed to a quarter past eight, as Mr Margrave's quiet brougham rolled up to her door.

Horace Margrave's professional position was no inconsiderable one. His practice was large and eminently respectable, lying principally amongst railway companies, and involving transactions of a very extensive kind. He was a man of excellent family, elegant, clever, and accomplished; too good for a lawyer, as everybody said; but a very good lawyer for all that, as his clients constantly repeated. At two-and-thirty he was still unmarried; why, no one could guess; as more than one great heiress, and many a pretty woman, would have been proud to say 'yes' to a matrimonial proposition from Horace Margrave, of Gray's Inn, and the Fir Grove, Stanleydale, Berkshire. But the handsome lawyer evidently preferred his free bachelor life; for if his heart had been very susceptible to womanly graces, he would most inevitably have lost it in the society of his lovely ward, Ellinor Arden.

Ellinor had only been a few weeks resident in London; she had left the guardianship of a maternal aunt in Paris, to launch herself upon the whirlpool of English society, sheltered only by the ample wing of an elderly lady, duly selected and chartered by her aunt and Mr Margrave. The world was new to her, and she came from the narrow circle of the convent in which she had been educated, and the quiet coteries of the faubourg Saint-Germain, in which her aunt delighted, to take her position at once in London, as the sole heiress of John Arden, of Arden.

It was then to Horace Margrave – to Horace Margrave, whom she remembered in her happy youth among the Scottish mountains, a young man on a shooting expedition, visiting at her father's house – Horace Margrave, who had visited her aunt from time to time, in Paris, and who exhibited towards her all the tender friendship of an elder brother – to him, and to him alone, did she look for counsel and guidance; and she submitted as entirely to his influence as if he had indeed been that guardian and father he by law represented.

Her cheek flushed as the carriage wheels stopped below the window.

'Now, Mrs Morrison,' she said with a sneer; 'now for my incomparable *futur*. Now for the light hair and thick boots.'

'It will be very ill-bred if he comes in thick boots,' replied her matter-of-fact chaperone. 'Mr Margrave says he is such an excellent young person.'

'Exactly, my dear Mrs Morrison – a young person. He is described in one word – a "person".'

'O, my dream, my dream!' she murmured under her breath.

She had but this day passed wisdom's Rubicon, and she was new to the hither bank.[2] She was still very romantic, and perhaps very foolish.

The servant announced 'Mr Margrave and Mr Dalton'.

In spite of herself, Ellinor Arden looked up with some curiosity to see this young man, for whom she entertained so profound a contempt and so unmerited an aversion. He was about three years her senior; of average height. His hair was, as she had prophesied, light; but it was by no means an ugly colour, and it framed a broad and massive forehead. His features were sufficiently regular; his eyes were dark blue. The expression of his face was grave, and it was only on rare occasions that a quiet smile played round his firmly-moulded lips. Standing side by side with Horace Margrave, he appeared anything but a handsome man; but to the physiognomist his face was superior in the very qualities in which the countenance of the lawyer was deficient – force, determination, self-reliance, perseverance; all those attributes, in short, which go to make a great man.

'Mr Dalton has been anxiously awaiting the hour that should bring him to your side, Miss Arden,' said Horace Margrave. 'He had been for a long time acquainted with those articles in your uncle's will which you only learned today.'

'I am sorry Miss Arden should have ever learned them, if they have given her pain,' said the young man quietly.

Ellinor looked up in his face, and saw that the blue eyes, looking down into hers, had a peculiar earnestness.

'He is not so bad, after all,' she thought. 'I have been foolish in ridiculing him; but I can never love him.'

'Miss Arden,' he continued, dropping into a chair by the sofa on which she was seated, while Horace Margrave leaned against the opposite side of the fireplace – 'Miss Arden, we meet under such peculiar circumstances, that it is best for the happiness of both that we should at once understand each other. Your late uncle was the dearest friend I ever had; no father could have been dearer to the most affectionate of sons than he was to me. Any wish, then, of his must be for ever sacred. But I have been brought up to rely upon myself alone, and can truly say I have no better wish than to make my own career, unaided by interest and fortune. The loss, then, of the money will be no loss to me. If it be your will to refuse my hand, and to retain the fortune to which you alone have a claim, do so. You shall never be disturbed in the possession of that to which you, of all others, have the best right. Mr Margrave, your solicitor and executor to your uncle's will, shall tomorrow execute a deed abnegating, on my part, all claim to this fortune; and I will, at one word from you, bid you adieu this night, before,' he added slowly, with an earnest glance at her beautiful face, – 'before my heart is too far involved to allow my being just to you.'

'Mr Dalton,' said Horace Margrave, lazily watching the two from under the shadows of his eyelashes, 'you bring Roman virtue into Mayfair. You will purify the atmosphere.'

'Shall I go or stay, Miss Arden?' asked the young man.

'Stay, Mr Dalton.' She rose as she spoke, and laid a hand, as if for support, upon the back of the chair that was standing near her. 'Stay, Mr Dalton. If your happiness can be made by the union, which was my late uncle's wish, let it be so. I cannot hold this fortune, which is not mine; but I may share it. I will confess to you, and I know your generous nature will esteem me better for the confession, that I have ventured to cherish a dream in which the image of another had a part. I have been foolish, mistaken, absurd; as schoolgirls often are. The dream is over. If you can accept my uncle's fortune and my own esteem; one is yours by right, the other has been won by your conduct of this evening.'

She held out her hand to him. He pressed it gently, raised it to his lips, led her back to the sofa, and reseated himself in the chair by her side.

Horace Margrave closed his eyes, as if the long-expected blow had fallen.

The rest of the evening passed slowly. Mr Margrave talked, and talked brilliantly; but he had a very dull audience. Ellinor was absent-minded, Henry Dalton thoughtful, and Mrs Morrison eminently stupid. The lawyer found it hard work to be brilliant in such dull company. When the clock, on which an ormolu Pan reclined amidst a forest of bronzed rushes, chimed the half-hour after ten, he carried away Mr Dalton; and Ellinor was left to ponder upon the solemn engagement into which she had entered on the impulse of the moment.

'I had better take a cab to the Temple,' said the young Dalton as they left the house. 'I'll wish you good night, Mr Margrave.'

'No, Mr Dalton, I have something to say to you that must be said, and which I think I'd rather say by night than by day. If you are not afraid of late hours, come home with me to my chambers, and smoke a cigar, I must have an hour's conversation with you before you see Ellinor Arden again. Shall it be tonight? I ask it as a favour; let it be tonight.'

Henry Dalton looked considerably astonished by the lawyer's words and manner; but he merely bowed, and said,

'With great pleasure. I am entirely at your service. If I returned to my chambers I should read for two or three hours, so pray do not be afraid of keeping me up.'

Henry Dalton and Horace Margrave sat talking for nearly three hours in the chambers of the latter; but no cigars were smoked by either or them, and though a bottle of Madeira stood on the table, it was untouched. It was to be observed, however, that a cellaret had been opened, and decanter of brandy taken out; the stopper lay beside it, and one glass, which had been drained to the dregs.

The clocks were striking two as Horace Margrave opened the outer door for his late visitor. On the threshold he paused, laid his hand, with a strong grasp, on Dalton's arm, and said in a whisper,

'I am safe, then! Your promise is sacred!'

Henry Dalton turned to him and looked him full in the face – looked full at the pale face and downcast eyes.

'The Daltons of Lincolnshire are not an aristocratic race, Mr Margrave; but they keep their word. Goodnight.'

He did not hold out his hand at parting, but merely lifted his hat and bowed gravely.

Horace Margrave sighed as he locked the doors, and returned to his warm study.

'At least,' he said, 'I am safe. But then I might have been happy. Have I been wise tonight? I wonder whether I have been wise,' he muttered, as his eyes wandered to a space over the mantelpiece, on which were arranged two pairs of magnificently mounted pistols, and a small dagger in a chased silver scabbard. 'Perhaps, after all, it was scarcely worth the trouble of this explanation; perhaps, after all, so miserable a game is scarcely worth the candle that lights it.'

3

AFTER THE HONEYMOON

Three months had elapsed since the midnight interview in Horace Margrave's chambers – three months, and the Opera House was opened for the season, and three new tenors, and two sopranos, and a basso-baritono had appeared under the classic proscenium of her Majesty's Theatre; and the novel of the season was in full circulation; Rotten Row was gay with Amazonian equestrians and blasé Life Guards men; moss roses were selling on the dusty pavements of the West End streets; and Covent Garden was all aglow with artistically-arranged bouquets, and all aglow with Algerian fruits; – London, in short, was in the full flood tide of the season, when Mr and Mrs Henry Dalton returned from their honeymoon visit to the Cumberland lake district, and took up their abode in the small house in Hertford Street furnished by Ellinor before her marriage.

Hers has been a short courtship; all the sweet uncertainties, the doubts, the dreams, the fears, the hopes which make up the poetical prologue to a love match, have been wanting in this marriage ordained by the will of her late uncle – this marriage, which is founded on esteem and not on affection; this marriage, into which she has entered on the generous impulse of an impetuous nature, which has never submitted itself to the discipline of reason.

Is she happy? Can this cold esteem, this calm respect which she feels for the man chosen for her by another, satisfy the ardent heart of the romantic girl?

She has been already married six weeks, and she has not seen Horace Margrave, the only friend she has in England – except, of course, her husband – since her wedding day; not since that sunny morning on which he took her icy hand in his and gave her, as her guardian and the representative of her dead father, into her husband's arms. She remembered that on that day when his hand touched hers it was as cold and nerveless as her own, and that his listless face was even paler than usual under the spring sunshine streaming in at the church windows. But in spite of this he did the honours of the breakfast table, toasted the bride and bridegroom, complimented the bridesmaids, and pleased everybody, with the finished grace and marvellous ease of the all-accomplished Horace Margrave. And if Ellinor had ever thought that she had a right, for auld lang syne, for her dead father's sake, or for her own lovely face, to be anything more or dearer to Mr Margrave than the most indifferent of his clients, that thought was dispelled by the most gentlemanly sangfroid of his adieu, as the four prancing steeds started off on the first stage to Windermere.

It was the end of June, and Mrs Dalton was seated in the small drawing room, awaiting the advent of morning visitors. Bridegroom and bride had been a week in town, and Horace Margrave had not yet called upon them. She had a weary air this morning, and sought in vain for something to occupy her. Now she strolled to the open piano, and played a few chords or a brilliant run, or softly touched the notes of some pensive air, and sang a few soft Italian syllables; now she took up an uncut novel from the table, and read a page or two here and there, wherever the book opened. Anon she walked to an embroidery frame, and took a great deal of trouble in selecting wools and threading needles; but when this was accomplished she did not work three stitches. After this she loitered listlessly about the room, looking at the pictures and proof engravings which adorned the pale silver-grey walls; but at last she sank into an easy chair by the open window, and sat idly looking down across a Lilliputian forest of heliotrope and geranium into the hot sunny street.

She was looking very lovely, but she was not looking happy. Her dark-brown hair was brushed away from her broad low brow, and secured in a coil of superb plaits at the back of her head; her white morning-dress was only ornamented by large knots of violet ribbon, and she wore no jewellery whatever, except a tiny, slender gold chain, which she twisted perpetually between her slim white fingers.

She sat thus for about half an hour, always looking across the plants in the balcony at the pavement opposite, when she suddenly wrenched the thin chain off her fingers.

She had seen the person for whom she had been waiting. A gentleman, who lounged along the other side of the street, crossed the road beneath the window, and knocked at the door.

'At last!' she muttered to herself; 'now, perhaps, this mystery will be explained.'

A servant announced Mr Margrave.

'At last!' she said again, rising as he entered the room. 'O, Mr Margrave, I have been so anxious to see you.'

He looked about on the crowded table to find amongst its fashionable litter a place for his hat; failed in doing so, and put it down on a chair; and then, for the first time, looked at his late ward.

'Anxious to see me, my dear Ellinor; why anxious?'

'Because there are two or three questions which I must ask, which you must answer.'

That peculiar expression in Horace Margrave's eyes, which was as it were a shiver of the eyelids, passed over them now; but it was too brief to be perceived by Ellinor Dalton. He sank into a chair; near her own, but not opposite to it. He paused to place his chair with its back to the light, and then said,

'My dear Ellinor – my dear Mrs Dalton – what questions can you have to ask me but questions of a purely business character; and even those I imagine your husband, who is quite as practical a man as myself, could answer as well as I?'

'Mr Dalton is the very last person to whom I can apply for an answer to the questions which I have to ask.'

'And why the last person?'

'Because those questions relate to himself.'

'O I see! My dear Mrs Dalton, is not this rather a bad beginning? You appeal from your husband to your solicitor.'

'No, Mr Margrave; I appeal to my guardian.'

'Pardon me, my dear Ellinor, there is no such person. He is defunct; he is extinct. From the moment I placed your hand in that of your husband before the altar of St George's, Hanover Square, my duties, my right to advise you, and your right to consult me, expired. Henceforth you have but one guardian, one adviser, one friend, and his name is Henry Dalton.'

A dark shadow came over Ellinor Dalton's face, and her eyes filled with tears as she said,

'Mr Margrave, Heaven forbid that I should say a word which could be construed in reproach to you. Your duties of guardianship, undertaken at the prayer of my dying father, have been as truly and conscientiously discharged as such duties should be discharged by a man of your high position and unblemished character. But I will own that sometimes, with a woman's folly, I have wished that, for the memory of my dead father, who loved and trusted you, for the memory of the old days in which we were companions and friends, some feeling a little warmer, a little kinder, a little more affectionate, something of the tenderness of an elder brother might have mingled with your punctilious fulfilment of the duties of guardian. I would not for the world reproach you, still less reproach you an act for which I only am responsible; yet I cannot but remember that, if it had been so, this marriage might never have taken place.'

'It is not a happy marriage, then?'

'It is a most unhappy one!'

Horace Margrave was silent for a few moments, and then began, gravely, almost sadly.

'My dear Mrs Henry Dalton,' – he seemed especially scrupulous in calling her Mrs Dalton, as if he had been anxious to remind her in every moment how much their relations had changed, – 'when you accuse me of a want of tenderness in my conduct towards yourself, of an absence of regard for the memory of your father, my kind and excellent friend, you accuse me of that for which I am no more responsible than for the colour of my hair, or the outline of my face. You accuse me of that which is perhaps the bane of my existence – a heart incapable of cherishing a strong affection, or sincere friendship, for any living being. Behold me, at five-and-thirty years of age, unloved and unloving, without one tie which I cannot as easily break as I can pay a hotel bill or pack my portmanteau. My life, at its brightest, is a dreary one – a dreary present, which can neither look back to a fairer past, nor forward to a happier future!'

His deep musical voice fell into a sadder cadence with these last words, and he looked down gloomily at the point of the cane with which he absently traced vague hieroglyphics upon the carpet. After a short silence, he looked up and said,

'But you wished to make some enquiries of me?'

'I did; I do. When I married Mr Dalton, what settlements were made? You told me nothing at that time, and I, so utterly unused to business matters, asked you no questions. Besides, I had then reason to think him the most honourable of men.'

'What settlements were made?' asked the lawyer, repeating Ellinor's question, as if it were the last of all others which he expected to hear.

'Yes; what arrangements were made about my fortune? How much of it was settled on myself?'

'Not one penny.'

Mrs Dalton gave a start of surprise, which Mr Margrave answered in his most nonchalant manner.

'Not one penny of it. There was no mention whatever of any such legal formality in your uncle's will. He left his money to you, but he left it to you only on condition that you shared it with his adopted son, Henry Dalton. This implied not only a strong affection for, but an implicit faith in, the young man. To tie up your money, or to settle it on yourself, would be to stultify your uncle's will. The man that could be trusted by him could be trusted by you. This is why I suggested no settlement. It is just possible that I acted in rather an unlawyer-like manner; but I believe that I acted in the only manner consonant with your late uncle's affectionate provisions for the two persons nearest and dearest to him.'

'Then Henry Dalton is the sole master of my – of the fortune?'

'As your husband, decidedly, yes.'

'And he may, if he pleases, sell the Arden estate?'

'The Arden estate is not entailed. Certainly he may sell it, if he wishes.'

'Then, Mr Margrave, I must inform you that he does wish to sell it, that he does intend to sell it.'

'To sell Arden Hall?'

'Yes.'

An angry flush crimsoned her face as she looked eagerly into the lawyer's eyes for one flash of surprise or indignation. She looked in vain.

'Well, my dear Mrs Dalton, in my opinion your husband shows himself a very sensible fellow by determining on such a proceeding. Arden is one of the dreariest, draughtiest, most dilapidated old piles of building in all England. It possesses all the leading features of a country mansion; magnificent oak panelling, contemptible servants' offices, three secret staircases, and not one register stove; six tapestried chambers, and no bathroom; a dozen Leonardo da Vincis, and not one door that does not let in assassination, in the shape of the north east wind; a deer park, and no deer; three gamekeeper's lodges and not game enough to tempt the more fatuitous of poachers! Sell Arden Hall! Nothing could be more desirable. But, alas, my dear Ellinor, your husband is not the man I take him for, if he calculates upon finding a purchaser.'

Mrs Dalton regarded the lawyer with not a little contempt, as she said,

'But the want of feeling, the outrage upon the memory of my poor uncle!'

'Your poor uncle will not be remembered a day the longer through your retaining possession of a draughty and uncomfortable house. When did Dalton tell you this intention of his?'

'On our return from our tour. I suggested that we should live there – that is, of course, out of season.'

'And he –?'

'Replied that it was out of the question our ever residing there, as the place must be sold.'

'You asked him his reasons?'

'I did. He told me that he was unable to reveal those reasons to me, and might never be able to reveal them. He said, that if

I loved him, I could trust him and believe in him, and believe that the course he took, however strange it might appear to me, was in reality the best and wisest course he could take.'

'But, in spite of this, you doubt him?' asked Horace earnestly.

'How can I do otherwise? He refuses me the slightest freedom in my use of the fortune which I have brought to him. He, the husband of a rich woman, enjoins economy – economy even in the smallest details. I dare not order a jewel, a picture, an elegant piece of furniture, a stand of hothouse flowers; for, if I do so, I am told that the expenditure is beyond his present means, and that I must wait till we have more money at our command. Then, again, his profession is a thousand times dearer to him than I. No brief-less, penniless barrister, with a mother and sister to support, ever worked harder than he works, ever devoted himself more religiously than he devotes himself to the drudging routine of the bar.'

'Ellinor Dalton, your husband is as high-minded and conscientious a man as ever lived upon this earth. I seldom take the trouble of making a vehement assertion; so believe me, if you can, now that I do. Believe me, even if you cannot believe him.'

'You too, against me?' cried Ellinor mournfully. 'O, believe me, it is not the money I want, it is not the possession of the money which I grudge him; it is only that my heart sinks at the thought of being united to a man I cannot respect or esteem. I did not ask to love him,' she added, half to herself; 'but I pray that I might be able to esteem him.'

'I can only say, Ellinor, that you are mistaken in him.'

At this same moment came the sound of a quick firm step on the stairs, and Henry Dalton himself entered the room.

His face was bright and cheerful, and he advanced to his wife eagerly; but at the sight of Horace Margrave he fell back with a frown.

'Mr Margrave, I thought it was part of our agreement that –'

The lawyer interrupted him.

'That I should never darken this threshold. Yes.'

Ellinor looked from one to the other with a pale, frightened face.

'Mr Dalton,' she exclaimed, 'what, in Heaven's name, does this mean?'

'Nothing that in the least that can affect you, Ellinor. A business disagreement between myself and Mr Margrave; nothing more.'

His wife turned from him scornfully, and approaching Horace Margrave, rested her hand on the scrollwork at the back of the chair on which he sat.

It was so small an action in itself, but it said, as plainly as words could speak, 'This is the man I trust, in spite of you, in spite of the world.'

It was not lost on Henry Dalton, who looked at this wife with a grave, reproachful glance, and said,

'Under these circumstances, then, Mr Margrave –'

'I had no right to come here. Granted; and I should not have come, but –'

He hesitated a moment, and Ellinor interrupted him.

'I wrote to my guardian, requesting him to call on me. Mr Dalton, what is the meaning of this? What mystery does all this conceal? Am I to see my best and oldest friend insulted in my own house?'

'A married woman has no friend but her husband: and I may not choose to receive Mr Margrave as a visitor in *our* house,' Henry Dalton replied, coldly and gravely.

'You shall not be troubled any longer with Horace Margrave's society, Mr Dalton,' said the lawyer rising, and walking slowly to the door.

'Good morning.'

His hand was upon the lock, when he turned, and with a tone of suppressed emotion addressed Mrs Dalton: 'Ellinor, shake hands with me,' he said. That was all. His sometime ward extended both her hands to him. He took them in his, bent his dark head over them for a moment as he held them in his grasp, and murmured hoarsely, 'Forgive me, Ellinor, and farewell.'

He was gone. She hurried out on to the landing-place, and called after him,

'Mr Margrave, guardian, Horace, come back! If only for one moment, come back!'

Her husband followed her, and led her back to the drawing room.

'Ellinor Dalton, choose between that man and me. Seek to renew your acquaintance with him, or hold any communication whatsoever with him that does not pass through my hands, and we part for ever.'

The young wife fell sobbing into her chair.

'My only friend!' she cried; 'my only, only friend! And to be parted from him thus!'

Her husband stood at a little distance from her, earnestly, sadly watching her, as she gave full sway to her emotion.

'What wretchedness! What utter wretchedness!' he said aloud; 'and no hope of a termination to it, no chance of an end to our misery.'

Henry Dalton prospered in his profession. Grey-headed old judges talked over their after-dinner port of the wonderful acumen displayed by the rising junior in the most important and difficult cases. One, two, three years passed away, and the name of Dalton began to be one of mark upon the Northern Circuit. The dawn often found him working in his chambers in Paper buildings, while his handsome wife was dancing at some brilliant assembly, or listening to the vapid platitudes of one of her numerous admirers and silent adorers. With Ellinor Dalton, to be unhappy was to be reckless. Hers was the impulsive and emotional nature which cannot brood upon its griefs in the quiet circle of a solitary home. She considered herself wronged by her husband's parsimony, still more deeply wronged by his cold reserve; and she sought in the gayest circles of fashionable London for the peace which had never dwelt at her cold and deserted hearth.

'His profession is all in all to him,' she said; 'but there is at least the world left for me; and if I cannot be loved I will prove to him that I can be admired.'

At many of the houses in which she was a constant visitor Horace Margrave was also a familiar guest. The wealthy bachelor lawyer was sure of a welcome wherever mamma had daughters to marry, and wherever pappa had money to invest or mortgages to effect. To her old guardian Ellinor's manner never underwent the shadow of a change.

'You may refuse to admit him here, you may forbid my correspondence with him. I acknowledge the right you exercise so harshly,' she would say to her husband; 'but you cannot shake my faith in my dead father's friend; you cannot control my sentiments towards the guardian of my childhood.'

But by degrees she found that Horace Margrave was to be seen less frequently every day at those houses in which she visited. It was growing a rare thing now for her to see the dark handsome head overtopping the crowd in which the lawyer mingled; and even when she did meet him, though his voice had still its old gentleness, there was a tacit avoidance of her in his manner, which effectually checked any confidence between them. This was for the first two years after her marriage. In the third she heard accidentally that Horace Margrave was travelling in Switzerland, and had left the entire management of his extensive business to a junior partner.

In the autumn of the third year, Ellinor was staying with her husband at the country house of his friend, Sir Lionel Baldwin. Since that day on which the scene with Horace Margrave had taken place in the little drawing room in Hertford Street, Ellinor Dalton and her husband had had no explanation whatsoever. On that day, the young man had fallen on his knees at the feet of his sobbing wife, and had most earnestly implored her to believe in his faith and honour, and to believe that, in everything he did, he had a motive so strong and so disinterested as to justify his conduct. He begged her to believe also that the marriage, on his part, had been wholly a love match; that he had been actuated by no mercenary considerations whatever; and that if he now withheld the money, to which, in all appearance, she had so good a right, it was because it was not in his power to lavish it upon her. But he implored in vain. Prejudiced against him from the very first, she had only trusted him for a brief period, to doubt him more completely than ever at the first suspicion that suggested itself. Wounded in her affection for another – an affection whose strength, perhaps, she scarcely dared to confess to herself – her feeling for Henry Dalton became one almost bordering on aversion. His simple, practical good sense; his plain, unpolished manners; his persevering, energetic, and untiring pursuit of a vocation with which she held no sympathy – all these qualities jarred upon her enthusiastic temperament, and blinded her to his actual merits. The world, which always contrives to know everything, very soon made itself completely acquainted with the eccentric conditions of Mr Arden's will, and the circumstances of Henry Dalton's marriage.

It was known to be a marriage of convenience, and not of affection. He was a very lucky fellow, and she was very much to be pitied. This was the general opinion, which Ellinor's palpable indifference to her husband went strongly to confirm.

Mr and Mrs Dalton had been staying for a week at Baldwin Court, when the young barrister was compelled, by his professional pursuits, to leave his wife for a few days under the protection of his old friends, Sir Lionel and Lady Baldwin.

'You will be very happy here, my dear Ellinor,' he said; 'the house is full of pleasant people, and you know what a favourite you are with the Baldwins. You will not miss me,' he added with a sigh, as he looked at her indifferent face.

'Miss you! O, pray do not alarm yourself, Mr Dalton! I am not so used to usurp your time or attention. I know, when your professional duties are concerned, how small a consideration I am to you.'

'I should not work hard were I not compelled to do so, Ellinor,' he said with a shade of reproach in his voice.

'My dear Mr Dalton,' she answered coldly, 'I have no taste for mysteries. You are perfectly free to pursue your own course.'

So they parted. She bade him adieu with as much well-bred indifference as if he had been her jeweller or her haberdasher.

As the light little phaeton drove him off to the railway station, he looked up to the chintz-curtained windows of his wife's apartments, and said to himself, 'How long is this to endure, I wonder? – this unmerited wretchedness, this cruel misconception.'

The morning after Henry Dalton's departure, as Sir Lionel Baldwin, seated at breakfast, opened the letter bag, he exclaimed, with a tone of mingled surprise and pleasure, 'So the wanderer has returned! At the very bottom of the bag I can see Horace Margrave's dashing superscription. He has returned to England.'

He handed his visitors their letters, and then opened his own, reserving the lawyer's epistle to the last.

'This is delightful! Horace will be down here tonight.'

Ellinor Dalton's cheek grew pale at the announcement; for the mysterious feud between her guardian and her husband flashed upon her mind. She would meet him here, then, alone. Now, or never, might she learn this secret – this secret which involved some meanness on the part of Henry Dalton, the apothecary's son.

'Margrave will be an immense acquisition to our party – will he not, gentlemen?' asked Sir Lionel.

'An acquisition! Well, really now, I don't know about that,' drawled a young government clerk from Whitehall. 'Do you know, Sir Lionel, it is my opinion that Horace Margrave is used up? I met him at – at what-you-may-call-it – Rousseau and Gibbon, *Childe Harold* and the *Nouvelle Héloïse*[3]: you know the place,' he said vaguely; 'somewhere in Switzerland, in short, – last July, and I never saw a man so altered in my life.'

'Altered!' exclaimed the Baronet.

Ellinor Dalton's face grew paler still.

'Yes, 'pon my honour, very much altered indeed. You don't think he ever committed a murder, or anything of that kind, do you?' said the young man reflectively, as he drew over a basin and deliberately dropped four or five lumps of sugar into his coffee. 'Because, upon my honour, he looked like that sort of thing.'

'My dear Fred, don't be a fool. Looked like what sort of thing?'

'You know; a guilty conscience – Lara, Manfred.[4] You understand. Upon my word,' added the youthful official, looking round with a languid laugh, 'he had such a Wandering-Jew-ish and ultra-Byronic appearance, when I met him suddenly among some very uncomfortable kind of chromolithographic mountain scenery, that I asked him if he had an appointment with the Witch of the Alps,[5] or any of that sort of people?'

One or two country visitors laughed faintly, seeing the young man meant to be jocose; and the guests from town only stared, as the government official looked around the table. Ellinor Dalton never took her eyes from his face, but seemed to wait anxiously for anything he might say next.

'Perhaps Margrave has been ill,' said the Baronet; 'he told me, when he went to Switzerland, that he was leaving England for change of air and scene.'

'Ill!' said the government clerk. 'Ah, to be sure; I never thought that. He might have been ill. It's difficult, sometimes, to draw the line between a guilty conscience and the liver complaint. Perhaps it was only his liver, after all. But you don't think,' he said appealingly, returning to his original idea, 'you don't think that he has committed a murder, and buried the body in Verulam buildings – do you? That would account for his going to Switzerland, you know; for he couldn't possibly stop with the body – could he?'

'You'd better ask him the question yourself, Fred,' said Sir Lionel, laughing; 'if everybody had as good a conscience as

Horace Margrave, the world would be better stocked than it is with honest men. Horace is a noble-hearted fellow; I've known him from a boy. He's a glorious fellow.'

'And a crack shot,' said a young military man with his mouth full of buttered toast and anchovy paste.

'And a first-rate billiard player,' added his next neighbour, who was occupied in carving a ham.

'And one of the longest-headed fellows in the *Law List*,' said a grave old gentleman sententiously.

'Extremely handsome,' faltered one young lady.

'And then, how accomplished!' ventured another.

'Then you don't think, really now, that he has committed a murder, and buried the body in his chambers?' asked the Whitehall employee, putting the question to the company generally.

In the dusk of that autumnal evening, Ellinor Dalton sat alone in a tiny drawing room leading out of the great saloon, which was a long room, with six windows and two fireplaces, and with a great many indifferent pictures in handsome frames.

This tiny drawing room was a favourite retreat of Ellinor's. It was deliciously furnished, and it communicated, by a half-glass door shrouded by cream-coloured damask curtains, with a large conservatory, which opened on to the terrace walk that ran along one side of the house. Here she sat in the dusky light, pensive and thoughtful, on the evening after her husband's departure. The gentlemen were all in the billiard room, hard at work with balls and cues, trying to settle some disputed wager before the half-hour bell rang to summon them to their dressing rooms. The ladies were already at their toilettes; and Ellinor, who had dressed earlier than usual, was quite alone. It was too dark for her to read or work, and she was too weary and listless to ring for lamps; so she sat with her hands lying idly in her lap, pondering upon the morning's conversation about Horace Margrave.

Suddenly a footstep behind her, falling softly on the thick carpet, roused her from her reverie, and she looked up with a startled glance at the glass over the low chimney piece.

In the dim firelight she saw, reflected in the shadowy depths of the mirror, the haggard and altered face of her some-time guardian, Horace Margrave.

He wore a loose overcoat, and had his hat in his hand. He had evidently only just arrived.

He drew back on seeing Ellinor, but as she turned to speak to him, the firelight behind her left her face in the shadow, and he did not recognise her.

'I beg your pardon,' he said, 'for disturbing you. I have been looking everywhere for Sir Lionel.'

'Mr Margrave! Don't you know me? It is I – Ellinor!'

The hat fell from Horace Margrave's slender hand, and he leaned against a high-backed easy chair for support.

'Ellinor – Mrs Dalton – you here! I – I – heard you were in Paris, or I should never – that is to say – I…'

For the first time in her life Ellinor Dalton saw Horace Margrave so agitated that the stony mask of gentlemanly sangfroid, which he ordinarily wore, dropped away, and revealed – himself.

'Mr Margrave,' she said anxiously, 'you are annoyed at seeing me here. O, how altered you are! They were right in what they said this morning, you are indeed altered; you must have been very ill!'

Horace Margrave was himself again. He picked up his hat, and sinking lazily into the easy chair upon which he had been leaning, said:

'Yes; I have had rather a severe attack – fever – exhaustion – the doctors, in fact, were so puzzled as to what they should call my illness, that they actually tried to persuade me that I had nerves – like a young lady who has been jilted by a Life Guards man, or forbidden by her parents to marry a country curate with seventy pounds per annum, and three duties every Sunday. A nervous lawyer! My dear Mrs Dalton, can you imagine anything so absurd? Sir James Clarke, however, insisted on my packing my portmanteau, and setting off for Mont Blanc, or something of that kind; and I, being heartily tired of the Courts of Probate and Chancery, and Verulam building, Gray's Inn, was only too glad to follow his advice, and take my railway ticket for Geneva.'

'And Switzerland has restored you?'

'In a measure; but not entirely. You can see that I am not yet very strong, when even the pleasing emotion of meeting unexpectedly with my sometime ward is almost too much for my nerves. But you were saying that they had been talking of me here.'

'Yes, at the breakfast table this morning. When your visit was announced, one of the gentlemen said he had met you in Switzerland, and that you were looking ill – unhappy!'

'Unhappy! Ah, my dear Mrs Dalton, what a misfortune it is for a man to have a constitutional pallor and a weak digestion! The world will insist upon elevating him into a blighted being, with a chronic wolf hard at work under his waistcoat. I knock myself up by working too hard over a difficult will case, in which some tiresome old man leaves his youngest son forty thousand pounds upon half a sheet of notepaper; and the world, meeting me in Switzerland, travelling to recruit myself, comes home and writes me down – unhappy. Now, isn't it too bad? If I were blessed with a florid complexion I might break my heart once in three months without any of my sympathetic friends troubling themselves about the fracture.'

'My dear Mr Margrave,' said Ellinor – her voice, in spite of herself, trembling a little – 'I am really now quite an old married woman; and, presuming on that fact, may venture to speak to you with entire candour – may I not?'

'With entire candour, certainly.' There was the old shiver in the dark eyelashes, and the old droop of the eyelids, as Horace Margrave said this.

'Then, my dear guardian, for I will – I will call you by the old name, which I can remember speaking for the very first time on the day of my poor father's funeral. O!' she added passionately, 'how well I remember that dreary day! I can see you now, as I saw you then, standing in the deep bay window in the library, in the dear, dear Scottish home, looking down at me so compassionately. I was such a child then. I can hear your low, deep voice, as I heard it on that day, saying to me – "Ellinor, your dead father has placed a solemn trust in my hands. I am young. I may not be so good a man as, to his confiding mind, I seemed to be; there may be something of constitutional weakness and irresolution in my character which he never suspected; but so deeply do I feel the trust implied in his dying words, that I swear, by my hope in Heaven, by my memory of the dead, by my honour as a gentleman, to discharge the responsibilities imposed upon me as an honest man should discharge them!"'

'Ellinor, Ellinor, for pity's sake!' cried the lawyer in a broken voice, clasping one wasted hand convulsively over his averted face.

'I do wrong,' she said, 'to recall that melancholy day; but I wanted to prove to you how your words were impressed upon my mind. You did, you did discharge every duty nobly, honestly, honourably; but now, now you abandon me entirely to the husband not of my choice, but imposed upon me by a cruel necessity, and you do all in your power to make us strangers. Yet, guardian – Horace, you are not happy!'

'Not happy!' he echoed, with a bitter laugh. 'My dear Mrs Dalton, this is such childish talk about happiness and unhappiness – two words which are only used in a lady's novel, in which the heroine is unhappy through two volumes and three quarters, and unutterably blest in the last chapter. In the practical world we don't talk about happiness and unhappiness; our phrases are failure and success. A man gets the woolsack, and he is successful; or he tries to earn bread and cheese, and fails, and we shrug our shoulders and say that he is unfortunate. But a happy man, my dear Ellinor – did you ever see one?'

'You mystify me; but you do not answer me.'

'Because to answer you I must first question myself; and, believe me, a man must have considerable courage who can dare to ask himself whether, in this troublesome journey of life, he has taken the right or the wrong road. I confess myself a coward, and implore you not to compel me to be brave.'

He rose, looked down at his dress, and exclaimed in his usual society tone,

'The first dinner-bell rang a quarter of an hour ago, and behold me still in travelling costume; the sin is yours, Mrs Dalton. Till dinner, adieu.'

It was difficult to recognise the gloomy and bitter Horace Margrave of the previous half-hour in the brilliant guest who sat on Lady Baldwin's right hand, and whose incessant flow of witty persiflage kept the crowded dinner table in a roar of laughter. Ellinor, charmed in spite of herself, beguiled out of herself by the fascination of his animated conversation, wondered at the extraordinary power possessed by this man.

'So brilliant, so accomplished!' she thought; 'so admired and successful, and yet so unhappy!'

That evening's post brought Ellinor a letter which had been sent to the house in Hertford Street, and forwarded thence to Sir Lionel's.

She started on seeing the direction and, taking her letter into the little inner drawing room, which was still untenanted, she read it by the light of the wax candles on the chimney piece. She returned to the long saloon after refolding the letter, crossed over to a small table at which Horace Margrave sat bending over a portfolio of engravings, seated herself near him, and said,

'Mr Margrave, I have just received a letter from Scotland.'

'From Scotland!'

'Yes. From the dear old clergyman, James Stewart; you remember him?'

'Yes; a white-headed old man with a family of daughters, the shortest of whom was taller than I. Do you correspond with him?'

'O, no. It is so many years since I left Scotland, that my old friends seem one by one to have dropped off. I should like so much to have given them a new church at Achindore; but Mr Dalton of course objected to the outlay of money, and as that is a point I never dispute with him, I abandoned the idea; but Mr Stewart has written to me this time for a special purpose.'

'And that is?'

'To tell me that my old nurse, Margaret Mackey, has become blind and infirm, and has been obliged to leave her situation. Poor dear old soul – she went into service in Edinburgh, after my poor father's death, and I entirely lost sight of her. I should have provided for her long before this had I known where to find her; but now there is no question about this appeal, and I shall immediately settle a hundred a year upon her, in spite of Mr Dalton's rigid and praiseworthy economy.'

'I fancy Mr Dalton will think a hundred a year too much. Fifty pounds for an old woman in the north of Aberdeenshire would be almost fabulous wealth. But you are so superb in your notions, my dear Ellinor. Hard-headed business men, like Dalton and myself, can scarcely stand against you.'

'Pray do not compare yourself to Mr Dalton,' said Ellinor coldly.

'I am afraid, indeed, I must not,' he answered with gravity; 'but you were saying…'

'That in this matter I will take no refusal; I will listen to no excuses or prevarications. I shall write to my husband by tomorrow's post. I cannot have an answer till the next day. If that answer should be either a refusal or an excuse, I know what course to take.'

'And that course…'

'I will tell you what it is when I receive Mr Dalton's reply. But I am unjust to him,' she said; 'he cannot refuse to comply with this request.'

Three days after this conversation, just as the half-hour bell had rung, and as Sir Lionel's visitors were hurrying off to their dressing rooms, Ellinor laid her hand lightly on Horace Margrave's arm, and said,

'Pray let me speak to you for a few minutes. I have received Mr Dalton's answer to my letter.'

'And that answer?' he asked as he followed her into the little room communicating with the conservatory.

'Is, as you suggested it might be, a refusal.'

'A refusal!' Mr Margrave elevated his eyebrows slightly, but seemed by no means surprised at the intelligence.

'Yes; a refusal. He dares not even attempt an excuse, or invent a reason for his conduct. Forty pounds a year, he says, will be a competence for an old woman in the north of Scotland, where very few ministers of the Presbyterian church have a larger income. That sum he will settle on her immediately, and he sends me a cheque for the first half-year; but he will settle no more, nor will he endeavour to explain motives which are always misconstrued. What do you think of his conduct?'

As she spoke, the glass door which separated the room from the conservatory swung backwards and forwards in the autumn breeze which blew in through the outer door of the conservatory. The day had been unusually warm for the time of year, and this outer door had been left open.

'My dear Ellinor,' said Horace Margrave, 'if anyone should come into this conservatory, they might hear us talking of your husband.'

'Everyone is dressing,' she answered carelessly. 'Besides, if anyone were there, they would scarcely be surprised to hear me declare my contempt for Henry Dalton. The world does not give us credit for being a happy couple.'

'As you will; but I am sure I heard someone stirring in that conservatory. But no matter. You ask me what I think of your husband's conduct in refusing to allow a superannuated nurse of yours more than forty pounds a year? Don't think me a heartless ruffian, if I tell you that I think he is perfectly right.'

'But to withhold from me my own money! To fetter my almsgiving! To control my very charities! I might forgive him if he refused me a diamond necklace or a pair of ponies; but in this matter, in which my affection is concerned, to let his economy step in to frustrate my earnestly expressed wishes – it is too cruel.'

'My dear Mrs Dalton, like all very impetuous and warm-hearted people, you are rather given to jump to conclusions. Mr Dalton, you say, withholds your own money from you. Now, your own money – with the exception of the Arden estate, which he sold within a year of your marriage – happens to have been entirely invested in the three percents. Now, suppose – mind, I haven't the least reason to suppose that such a things has ever happened, but for the sake of putting a case – suppose Henry Dalton, as a clever and enterprising man of business, should have been tempted to speculate with some of your money?'

'Without consulting me?'

'Without consulting you. Decidedly. What do women know of speculation?'

'Mr Margrave, if Henry Dalton has done this, he is no longer a miser, but he is – a cheat. The money bequeathed to me by my uncle was mine: to be shared with him, it is true, but still mine. No sophistry, no lawyer's quibble, could ever have made it his. If, then, he has, without my consent or knowledge, speculated with that money, he is a dishonest man. Ah, Horace Margrave, you, who have noble blood in your veins – you, who are a gentleman, an honourable man – what would you think of Henry Dalton, if this were possible?'

'Ellinor Dalton, have you ever heard of the madness men have christened gambling? Do you know what a gambler is? Do you know what the man feels who hazards his wife's fortune, his widowed mother's slender pittance, his helpless children's inheritance, the money that should pay for his son's education, his daughter's dowry, the hundreds due to his trusting creditors, or the gold entrusted to him by a confiding employer, – on the green cloth of a west end gaming table? Do you think that at that mad moment, when the glaring lights above the table dazzle his eyes, and the piles of gold heave up and down upon the green baize, and the croupier's voice crying, "Make your game!" is multiplied by a million, and deafens his bewildered ear like the clamour of all the fiends; do you think at that moment that he ever supposes he is going to *lose* the money? No; he is going to double, to treble, to quadruple it; to multiply every guinea by a hundred, and to take it back to the starving wife or the anxious children, and cry, "Was I so much to blame, after all?" Have you ever stood upon the grandstand at Epsom, and seen the white faces of the betting men, and heard the roar of the eager voices at the last rush for the winning post? Every man upon that crowded stand, every creature upon that crowded course – from the great magnate of the turf, who stands to win a quarter of a million, to the wretched apprentice lad, who has stolen half a crown from the till to put it upon the favourite – believes that he has backed a winning horse. That is the great madness of gaming; that is the terrible witchcraft of the gambling house and the ring; and that is the miserable hallucination of the man who speculates with the fortune of another. Pity him, Ellinor. If the weak and the wicked are ever worthy of the pity of the good, that man deserves your pity.'

He had spoken with an energy unusual to him, and he sank into a chair, half exhausted by his unwonted vehemence.

'I would rather think the man whom I am forced to call my husband a miser than a cheat, Mr Margrave,' Ellinor said coldly, 'and I am sorry to learn, that if he were indeed capable of such dishonour, his crime would find an advocate in you.'

'You are pitiless, Mrs Dalton,' said Horace Margrave, after a pause. 'God help the man who dares to wrong you!'

'Do not let us speak of Henry Dalton any longer, Mr Margrave. I told you that if he should refuse this favour, this – this right, I had decided on my course.'

'You did; and now, may I ask what that course is?'

'To leave him.'

'Leave him!' he exclaimed anxiously.

'Yes; leave him in the possession of the money which is so dear to him. He can never have cared for me. He has refused my every request, frustrated my every wish, devoted every hour of his life, not to me, but to his profession. My aunt will receive me. I shall leave this place tonight, and leave London for Paris tomorrow morning.'

'What will the world say to such a step, Ellinor?'

'Let the world judge between us. What can the world say of me? I shall live with my aunt, as I did before my luckless inheritance came to me. Mr Margrave – guardian – you will accompany me to Paris, will you not? I am so inexperienced in all these sorts of things, so little used to help myself, that I dare not make the journey with my maid alone. You will accompany me?'

'I, Ellinor?'

'Yes; who so fit to protect me as you, to whom, with his dying lips, my father committed my guardianship? For his sake you will do me this service, will you not?'

'Is it a service, Ellinor? Can I be doing you a service in taking you away from your husband?'

'So be it, then,' she said scornfully. 'You refuse to help me; I will go alone.'

'Alone?'

'Yes, alone; I go tonight, and alone.'

A crimson flush mounted to Horace Margrave's pale face, and a vivid light shone in his handsome eyes.

'Alone, Ellinor? No, no,' he said; 'my poor child, my ward, my helpless orphan girl, my little Scotch lassie of the good time gone, I will protect you on this journey, place you safely in the arms of your aunt, and answer to Henry Dalton for my conduct. In this at least, Ellinor, I will be worthy of your dear father's confidence. Make your arrangements for the journey. Have you your maid with you?'

'Yes; Ellis, a most excellent creature. Then tonight, by the mail train.'

'I shall be ready. You must make your excuses to Lady Baldwin, and leave me with as little explanation as possible. Au revoir!'

As Ellinor Dalton and Horace Margrave left the little boudoir, a gentleman in a greatcoat, with a railway rug flung over his shoulder, strode out on to the terrace through the door of the conservatory, and lighting a cigar, paced for about half an hour up and down the shrubbery at the side of the house, wrapped in thought.

5

FROM LONDON TO PARIS

While dressing, Ellinor gave her maid orders to set about packing, immediately. Ellis, a solemn and matter-of-fact person, expressed no surprise, but went quietly to work, emptying the contents of wardrobes into capacious trunks, and fitting silver-topped bottles into their velvet-lined cases, as if there were no such thing as hurry or agitation in the world.

To Ellinor Dalton that evening seemed very long. Never had the county families appeared so stupid, or the London visitors so tiresome. The young man from the War Office took her in to dinner, and insisted on telling her some very funny story about a young man in another government office, which brilliant anecdote lasted, exclusive of interruptions, from the soup to dessert, without drawing any nearer the point of the witticism. After the dreary dinner, the eldest daughter of the oldest of the county families fastened herself and a very difficult piece of crochet upon her, and inflicted on her all the agonies of a worsted-work rose, which, as the young lady perpetually declared, would not come right. But however distraite Ellinor might be, Horace Margrave was the Horace of the West End world. He talked politics with the heads of the county families; stock exchange with the city men; sporting magazine and Tattersall's with the county swells; discussed the latest debuts at her Majesty's Theatre with the young Londoners; spoke of Sir John Herschel's last discovery to a scientific country squire; and of the newest thing in farming implements to an agricultural ditto; talked compliments to the young country ladies, and the freshest Mayfair scandal to the young London ladies; had, in short, something to say on every subject to everybody, and contrived to please all. And let any man who has tried to do this in the crowded drawing room of a country house, say whether or not Horace Margrave was a clever fellow.

'By the by, Horace,' said Sir Lionel, as the lawyer lounged against one corner of the mantelpiece, talking to a group of young men and one rather fast young lady, who had edged herself into the circle, under cover of a brother, much to the indignation of more timid spirits, who sat modestly aloof, furtively regarding Admirable Crichton Margrave, as his friends called him, from distant sofas; 'by the by, my boy, where did you hide yourself this morning? We sadly wanted you to decide a match at billiards, and I sent people all over the house and grounds in search of you.'

'I rode over to Horton after lunch,' said Horace. 'I wanted a few hours there on electioneering business.'

'You've been to Horton?' asked Sir Lionel, with rather an anxious expression.

'Yes, my dear Sir Lionel, to Horton. But how alarmed you look! I trust I haven't been doing anything wrong. A client of mine is going to stand for the place. But surely you're not going to throw over the county electors, and stand for the little borough of Horton yourself!' he said, laughing.

'Why, how silent everyone has grown!' said Horace, still laughing. 'It seems as if I had launched a thunderbolt upon this hospitable hearth, in announcing my visit to the little manufacturing town of Horton. What is it – why is it – how is it?' he asked looking round with a smile.

'Why,' said Sir Lionel hesitantly, 'the – the truth of the matter – that is – not to mystify you – in short – you know – they, they've a fever at Horton. The – the working classes and factory people have got it very badly, and – and – the place is in a manner *tabooed*. But of course,' added the old man, trying to look cheerful, 'you didn't go into any of the back streets, or amongst the lower classes. You only rode through the town, I suppose; so you're safe enough, my dear Horace.'

The county families simultaneously drew a long breath, and the young lady in pink released her sister's wrist.

'I went, my dear Sir Lionel,' said Horace, with placid indifference, 'into about twenty narrow back streets in an hour and a half, and I talked to about forty different factory hands, for I wanted to find which way the political current set in the good town of Horton. They all appeared extremely dirty, and now, I remember, a good many of them looked ill; but I'm not afraid of having caught the fever, for all that,' he added, looking round at the grave faces of his hearers; 'half a dozen cigars, and a sharp ten miles' ride through a bleak, open country must be a thorough disinfectant. If not,' he continued bitterly, 'one must die sooner or later, and why not of a fever caught at Horton?'

The young lady in pink had recourse to her sister's wrist again at this speech.

Horace soon laughed off the idea of danger from his afternoon's rambles, and, in a few minutes, he was singing a German student song, and accompanying himself at the piano.

At last the long evening was over, and Ellinor, who had heard nothing from her distant worktable of the conversation about the fever, gladly welcomed the advent of the servant with a tray of glistening candlesticks. As she lit her candle at the side table, Horace Margrave came over, and lit his own.

'I have spoken to Sir Lionel,' he said; 'a carriage will be ready for us in an hour. The London mail does not start till one o'clock, and we shall reach town in time to catch the day service to Paris. But, Ellinor, it is not yet too late. Are you thoroughly determined on this step?'

'Thoroughly,' she said. 'I shall be ready in an hour.'

Mrs Dalton's apartments were at the end of a long corridor; the dressing room opened out of the bedroom, and the door of communication was ajar as Ellinor entered her room. Her boxes stood ready packed. She looked at them hurriedly, examined the addresses which her maid had pasted upon them, and was about to pass into the dressing room, when she stopped on the threshold with an exclamation of surprise.

Henry Dalton was seated at the table, with an open portfolio spread before him, writing busily. On a chair by the fire lay his greatcoat, a railway rug, and portmanteau.

He looked up for a moment, calmly and gravely, as Ellinor entered; and then continued writing.

'Mr Dalton!'

'Yes,' he said, still writing; 'I came down by the 5.30 train. I returned sooner than I expected.'

'By the 5.30 train,' she said anxiously; 'by the train which leaves London at half past five, I suppose?'

'By the train which arrives here at half past five,' answered her husband, without looking up; 'or should reach here by that time, rather; for it's generally five minutes late.'

'You have been here since six o'clock?'

'Since ten minutes to six, my dear Ellinor. I gave my valise to the porter, and walked over from the station in a quarter of an hour.'

'You have been here since six, yet you have neither told me of your arrival nor shown yourself in the house!'

'I have shown myself to Sir Lionel. I had some very important business to arrange.'

'Important business?' she asked.

'Yes, to prepare for this journey to Paris, which you are so bent upon taking.'

'Mr Dalton!'

'Yes,' he said quietly, folding and sealing a letter as he spoke, 'it is very contemptible, is it not? Coming unexpectedly into a house by the conservatory entrance – which, as you know, to anyone arriving from the station, saves about two hundred yards – I heard involuntarily a part of a conversation, which had so great an effect upon me as to induce me to remain where I was, and voluntarily hear the remainder.'

'A listener?' she said with a sneer.

'Yes, it is on a par with all the rest, is it not? An avaricious man, a money-grabbing miser; or, perhaps, even worse, a dishonest speculator. O, Ellinor Dalton, if ever the day should come (God forbid that I should wish to hasten it by an hour!) when I shall be free to speak one little sentence, how bitterly you will regret your expressions of today! But I do not wish to reproach you: it is our bad fortune – yours and mine – to be involved in a very painful situation, from which, perhaps, nothing but an open rupture could extricate us. You have taken the initiative. You wish to leave me, and return to your aunt in Paris. So be it. Go.'

'Mr Dalton!'

Something in his manner, in spite of her long-cherished prejudices against him, impressed and affected her, and she stretched out her hand deprecatingly.

'Go, Ellinor! I, too, am weary of this long struggle! This long conflict with appearances which, in spite of myself, condemn me. I am sick to the very heart of these perpetual appeals to your generosity and confidence – tired of trying to win the love of a woman who despises me.'

'But, Henry, if – if – I have misconstrued –' she said, with a tenderness unusual to her in addressing her husband.

'*If* you have misconstrued –' he exclaimed passionately. 'No, Ellinor, no; it is too late now for explanations; besides I could give you none better than those you have already heard – too late for reconciliation; the breach has been slowly widening for three long years; and tonight I look at you across an impassable abyss, and wonder that I could have ever dreamed, as I have dreamed, of ultimately winning your love.'

There was a break in his voice as he said these last words, and the emotion, so strange to the ordinary manner of the young barrister, melted Ellinor.

'Mr Dalton! Henry!'

'You wish to go to Paris, Ellinor. You shall go. But the man who accompanies you thither must be Henry Dalton.'

'You will take me there?' she asked.

'Yes; and I will place you under your aunt's protection. From that moment you are free of me for ever. You will have about three hundred a year to live upon. It is not much out of the three thousand, is it?' he said, laughing bitterly; 'but I give you my honour it is all I can afford, as I shall want the rest for myself.' He looked at his watch. 'A quarter-past twelve,' he said. 'Dress yourself warmly, Ellinor; it will be a cold journey. I will ring for the people to take your trunks down to the carriage.'

'But, Henry,' she took his hand in hers; 'Henry, something in your manner tonight makes me think that I have wronged you. I won't go to Paris. I will remain with you; I will trust you.'

He pressed the little hand lying in his very gently, and said, looking at her gravely and sadly, with thoughtful blue eyes,

'*You cannot*, Ellinor! No, no; it is far better, believe me, as it is, I have borne the struggle for three years. I do not think that I could endure it for another day. – Ellis?' he said, as the maid entered the room in answer to his summons, 'you will see that this letter is taken to Mr Margrave immediately, and then see that those trunks are carried downstairs. – Now, Ellinor, if you are ready.'

She stopped in the hall, and said,

'I must say goodbye to Mr Margrave, and explain this change in our plans.'

'My letter has done that, Ellinor. You will not speak one word to Horace Margrave while I am beneath this roof.'

'As you will,' she answered submissively.

She had suddenly learned to submit to, if not to respect, her husband.

Henry Dalton was very silent during the short drive to the railway station; and when they alighted, he said:

'You would like to have Ellis with you, would you not?'

Ellinor assented, and her maid followed her into the carriage. It seemed as if her husband had been anxious to avoid a tête-à-tête.

Throughout the four hours' journey Ellinor found herself involuntarily watching the calm, grave face of her husband under the dim carriage lamp. It was impossible to read any emotion on that smooth brow, or in those thoughtful eyes, but she remembered the agitation as he spoke to her in her dressing room.

'He is capable of some emotion,' she thought. 'What if after all I should really have wronged him? If there should be some other key to this strange mystery than meanness and avarice? If he really loves me, and I have misconstrued him, what a wretch he must think me!'

The next evening, after dark, they arrived in Paris; and Ellinor found herself, after an interval of nearly four years, once more in her aunt's little drawing room in the rue Saint-Dominique. She was received with open arms. Henry Dalton smoothed over the singularity of her arrival, by saying that it was a visit of his own suggestion.

'Everything will explain itself at a future time, Ellinor; for the present, let ours be thought a temporary separation. I do not wish to alarm your poor aunt.'

'You shall have your own old bedroom, Ellinor,' said her aunt. 'Nothing has been disturbed since you left us – look;' and she opened the door of a little apartment leading out of the drawing room, in which ormolu clocks, looking glasses, and pink curtains very much preponderated over more substantial furniture.

'But you are looking very ill, my dear child,' she said anxiously as Ellinor pushed away the untasted refreshment which her aunt had ordered for her, – 'you are really looking very ill!'

'My journey has fatigued me a little. I think I'll go to my room at once, if you will excuse me, aunt; it is nearly eleven o'clock.'

'Yes; and rest will do you more good than anything. Good night, my darling child. Lisette is getting your room ready.'

Wearied out with a night and a day of incessant travelling, Ellinor slept soundly, and waking the next morning, found her aunt seated by her bedside.

'My dear girl, you look a great deal better after your night's rest. Your husband would not disturb you to say goodbye, but has left this letter for you.'

'Has Mr Dalton gone?'

'Yes; he said he had most important business – something about his circuit,' said her aunt vaguely; 'but his letter will no doubt explain all. He has made every arrangement for your comfort during your stay with me, dear. He seems a most devoted husband.'

'He is very good,' said Ellinor with a sigh. Her aunt left her, and she opened the letter – opened it with an anxiety she could not repress. She hoped this letter might contain some explanation, some offer of reconciliation.

My Dear Ellinor,

When you receive these few lines of farewell, I shall be on my way to London. In complying with your wish, and restoring you to the home of your youth, I hope and believe that I have acted for the best. How completely you have misunderstood me, how entirely you have mistaken my motives, you may never know. How much I have suffered from this wretched misunderstanding it would be impossible for me to tell you. But let this bitter past be forgotten; our roads in life henceforth lie separate. Yet if at any future hour you should need an adviser or an earnest and disinterested friend, I entreat you to appeal to no one but

Henry Dalton

The letter fell from her hand.

'Now, now I am indeed alone,' she thought.

6

HORACE MARGRAVE'S CONFESSION

Life in the faubourg Saint-Germain seemed very dreary to Ellinor after the pleasant London society to which she had been accustomed since her marriage. Her aunt's visiting list was very limited. Four or five ancient dowagers, who thought that the glory of the world had departed with the Bourbons, and that France, in the van of that great march of civilisation, was the foremost in a demoniac species of dance, leading only to destruction and the erection of a new guillotine upon the place de la Révolution; two or three elderly but creditably-preserved aristocrats of the *ancien régime*, whose political principles had stood still ever since the Restoration, and who resembled ormolu clocks of that period, very much ornamented and embellished, but useless as indicators of the flight of times; three or four very young ladies educated in convents, and uninterested in anything except their pet priests and the manufacture of point-lace; and one terrifically bearded and moustachioed gentleman, who had written a volume of poems entitled *Clouds and Mists*, but who had not yet been so fortunate as to meet with a publisher, – this was about the extent of the visiting circles in the rue Saint-Dominique; and for this circle Ellinor's aunt set apart a particular day, on which she was visible in conjunction with *eau sucrée*, rather weak coffee, and wafer biscuits.

The first day of Ellinor's visit happened to be the day of her aunt's reception, and it seemed to her as if the tiresome hours would never wear themselves out, or the equally tiresome guests take their departure. She could not help remembering how different everything would have been had Horace Margrave been present. How he would have fought the battle of the *tiers état* with the white-headed old partisans of the departed noblesse; how he would have discussed and critically analysed Lamartine's odes with the young ladies from the convent; how he would have flattered the vanity of the bearded poet, and regretted the Bourbons with the faded old dowagers. But he was away – gone out of her life, perhaps, entirely.

'I shall never see him again,' she said; 'that kind guardian in whose care my father left me.'

The next day she went with her aunt to the Louvre to see the improvements that had been made beneath the sway of the new ruler who had already begun to change brick into marble, or at least into stucco. The pictures only wearied her; the very colouring of the Rubenses seemed to have lost half its glowing beauty since she had last seen them; and Marie de Medici, florid and resplendent, bored her terribly. Many of the recent acquisitions she thought overrated, and she hurried her aunt away from the splendid exhibition before they had been there an hour. She made a few purchases in the rue de la Paix; and loitered for a little time at a milliner's in the rue de l'Échelle, choosing a bonnet, and then declared herself thoroughly tired with the morning's exertions.

She threw herself back in the carriage, and was very silent as they drove home; but suddenly, as they turned from the rue du Rivoli into the quadrangle of the Louvre, they passed close to a hackney coach in which a gentleman was seated, and Ellinor, starting up, cried out,

'It was Mr Margrave! Did you not see him, aunt? He has just this moment passed us in a hackney coach.'

She pulled the check-string violently as she spoke, and her aunt's coachman stopped, but Horace Margrave was out of sight, and the vehicle in which he was seated lost among the crowd of carriages of the same description rattling up and down the bustling street.

'Never mind, dear,' said Miss Beauchamp, as Ellinor let down the carriage window, and looked eagerly out; 'if you are not mistaken in the face of the person who passed us, and it really is Horace Margrave, he is sure to call upon us immediately.'

'Mistaken in my guardian's face! No, indeed. But of course he will call, as you say, aunt.'

'Yes; he will call this evening, most likely. He knows how seldom I go out.'

All that evening and all the next morning Mrs Dalton constantly expected to hear the lawyer's name announced; but he did not come.

'He had important business to transact yesterday, perhaps,' she thought; 'and he may be employed this morning; but in the evening he is sure to call.'

After dinner she sat by the low wood fire in Miss Beauchamp's drawing room, turning over the leaves of a book which she had vainly endeavoured to read, and looking every moment at the old buhl[6] clock over the chimney; but the evening slowly dragged itself through, and still no Horace Margrave. She expected him on the following day, but again only to be disappointed; and in this manner the week passed, without bringing any tidings of him.

'He must have left Paris!' she thought; 'left Paris, without once calling here to see me. Nothing could better testify his indifference,' she added bitterly. 'It was no doubt only for my father's sake that he ever pretended any interest in the friendless orphan girl.'

The following week, Ellinor went with her aunt once or twice to the Opera, and to two or three réunions in the

59

faubourg; at which her handsome face and elegant manners made some sensation; but still there were no tidings of Horace Margrave.

'If he had been in Paris, we should most likely have seen him at the Opera,' thought Ellinor.

That week elapsed, and on the Sunday evening Mrs Dalton sat alone in her own room, writing letters to friends in England, when she was interrupted by a summons from her aunt. Some-one wanted her in the drawing room immediately.

Someone in the drawing room who wanted to see her! Could it be her guardian at last?

'A lady or a gentleman?' she asked of the servant who brought her aunt's message.

'A lady – a sister of charity.'

She hurried into the drawing room, and found a sister of charity in conversation with Miss Beauchamp.

'My dear Ellinor, this lady wishes you to accompany her on a visit to a sick person; a person whom you know, but whose name she is forbidden to reveal. What can this mystery mean?'

'A sick person wishes to see me?' said Ellinor. 'But I know so few people in Paris; no one likely to send for me.'

'If you can trust me, madame,' said the nun, 'and if you will accompany me on my visit to this person, I believe your pres-ence will be of great service. The mind of the invalid is, I regret to say, in a very disturbed state, and you only I imagine, will be able, under Heaven and the church, to give relief to that.'

'I will come,' said Mrs Dalton.

'But, Ellinor –' exclaimed her aunt anxiously.

'If I can be of any service, my dear aunt, it would be most cruel, most cowardly, to refuse to go.'

'But, my dear child, when you do not know the person to whom you are going.'

'I will trust this lady,' answered Ellinor, 'and I will go. – I will put on my bonnet and shawl, and join you, madame,' she added to the nun, as she hurried from the apartment.

'When these girls once get married, there's no managing them,' murmured Miss Beauchamp, as she folded her thin white hands, bedecked with old-fashioned rings, resignedly. 'Pray do not let them detain her long,' she continued aloud, to the sister of charity, who sat looking gravely into the few embers in the little English grate. 'I shall suffer the most excruciating anxiety till I see her safe home again.'

'She will be perfectly safe with me, madame.'

'Now, madame, I am quite at your service,' said Ellinor, re-entering the room.

In a few minutes they were seated in a hackney coach, and rattling through the quiet faubourg.

'Are we going far?' asked Ellinor of her companion.

'To Meurice's Hotel.'

'To Meurice's? Then the person I am going to see is not a resident in Paris?'

'No, madame.'

Who could it be? Not a resident in Paris. Someone from England, no doubt. Her husband, or Horace Margrave? These were the only two persons who presented themselves to her mind; but in either case, why this mystery?

They reached the hotel, and the sister of charity herself led the way upstairs into an enclosed hall on the third story, where she stopped suddenly at the door of a small sitting room, which she entered, followed by Ellinor.

Two gentlemen, evidently medical men, stood talking in whispers, in the embrasure of the window. One of them looked up as the two women entered, and to him the nun said,

'Your patient, Monsieur Delville?'

'He is quieter, Sister Louise. The delirium has subsided; he is now quite himself; but very much exhausted,' replied the physician. 'Is this the lady?' he asked, looking at Ellinor.

'Yes, monsieur.'

'Madame,' said the doctor, 'will you favour me with a few moments' conversation?'

'With pleasure, monsieur. But first, let me implore you, one word. This sick person, for mercy's sake, tell me his name!'

'That I cannot do, madame; his name is unknown to me.'

'But the people in the hotel?'

'Are also ignorant of it. His portmanteau has no address. He came most probably on a flying visit; but has been detained here by a very alarming illness.'

'Then let me see him, monsieur. I cannot endure this suspense. I have reason to suppose that this gentleman is a friend who is very dear to me. Let me see him, and then I shall know the worst.'

'You shall see him, madame, in ten minutes. Monsieur Vernot, will you prepare the patient for an interview with this lady?'

The second doctor bowed gravely, and withdrew into an inner apartment, closing the door carefully behind him.

'Madame,' said Monsieur Delville, 'I was called in, only three days ago, to see the person lying in the next room. My colleague had been for some time attending him through a very difficult case of typhus fever. A few days ago the case became still more complicated and difficult by an affection of the brain which supervened, and Monsieur Vernot considered it his duty to call in another physician. I was therefore summoned. I found the case, as my colleague had found it, an exceptional one. There was not only physical weakness to combat, but mental depression – mental depression of so marked a character that both Monsieur Vernot and myself feared that, should we even succeed in preserving the life of the patient, we might fail in saving his reason.'

'How dreadful, how dreadful!' murmured Ellinor.

'During the three days and nights in which I have attended him,' continued the doctor, 'we have not succeeded until this evening in obtaining an interval in consciousness; but throughout the delirium our patient has perpetually dwelt upon two or three subjects, which, though of a different character, may be by some chain of circumstances connected into the one source of his great mental wretchedness. Throughout his wanderings one name has been incessantly upon his lips.'

'And that name is –'

'Ellinor Dalton.'

'My own name.'

'Yes, madame, your name, coupled with perpetual entreaties for pardon; for forgiveness of a great wrong – a wrong long since, and artfully concealed –'

'A wrong done! If this gentleman is the person I suspected him to be, he never was anything but the truest friend to me. But, for pity's sake, let me see him. This suspense is unbearable.'

'One moment, madame. I had some difficulty in finding you; but mentioning the name of the lady of whom I was in search, I fortunately happened to make the inquiry of a friend of Miss Beauchamp. This good, devoted Sister Louise, here, was ready to set out immediately on her errand of mercy, and I thought that you might feel, perhaps, more confidence in her than in me.'

At this moment the door of communication between the two apartments was softly opened, and Monsieur Vernot returned.

'I have prepared the patient for your visit, madame,' he said; 'but you must guard against a shock to your own feelings in seeing him. He is very ill.'

'In danger?' asked Ellinor.

'Unhappily, yes – in imminent danger!'

Throughout the brief interview with the physician Ellinor Dalton had said to herself, 'Whatever it is that must be endured by me, I will bear it bravely; for his sake I will bear it bravely.' Her face was white as death – the firm, thin lips locked over the closely-shut teeth – the mournful grey eyes tearless and serene; but her heart beat so loudly, that she seemed to hear its every pulsation in the stillness of the room.

Her worst presentiments were realised.

Horace Margrave lay with his head thrown back upon the piled-up pillows, and his attenuated hand stretched listlessly upon the dark silk counterpane. His head was bound with wet linen, over which his nurse had tied a handkerchief of scarlet, whose vivid hue made his ashen face still more ghastly. His dark eyes had lost the dreamy expression usual to them, and had the feverish lustre of disease. They were fixed, with a wild haggard gaze, upon the door through which Ellinor entered.

'At last!' he said, with a hysterical cry; 'at last!'

Ellinor sank on her knees by his bedside, and said to him, very quietly,

'Horace, what is this? Why do I find you thus?'

He fixed his haggard eyes upon her, as she answered,

'What is it, Ellinor! Shall I tell you?'

'Yes, yes; if you can tell me without unnerving yourself.'

'Unnerving myself!' he cried, with a bitter laugh. 'Unnerve myself – look at that!' He stretched out one thin, semi-transparent hand, which trembled like an aspen leaf, until he let it fall lifelessly upon the quilt. 'For four years, Ellinor, I have been slowly burning out my life in one long nervous fever. And you tell me not to unnerve myself!'

He gave a restless, impatient sigh, tossed his weary head back upon the pillow, and turned his face to the wall.

Ellinor Dalton looked around the room in which this all-accomplished, admired, and prosperous Horace Margrave had lain for eleven dreary days, eleven painful nights.

It was a small apartment, comfortably furnished, and heated by a stove. On the table by the bedside a *Book of Hours* lay open, with a rosary thrown across the page where the reader had left off. Near this was an English Testament, also lying open. The nun who had been nursing Horace Margrave had procured this English Gospel, in hopes that he would be induced to read it. But the sick man, when sensible, spoke to her in French; and when she implored him to see a priest, refused, with an impatient gesture, which he repeated when she spoke to him of a Protestant clergyman whom she knew, and could summon to him.

The dim lamp was shaded from the eyes of the invalid by a white porcelain screen, which subdued the light, and cast great shadows of the furniture upon the walls of the room.

He lay for some time quite still, with his face averted; but by the incessant nervous motion of the hand lying upon the counterpane, Mrs Dalton knew that he was not asleep.

The doctor opened the door softly, and looked in.

'If he says anything to you,' he whispered to Ellinor, 'hear it quietly; but do not ask him any questions; and, above all, betray no agitation.'

She bowed her head in assent, and the physician closed the door.

Suddenly Horace Margrave turned his face towards her, and, looking at her with earnest scrutinising eyes, said,

'Ellinor Dalton, you ask me what this means. I will tell you. The very day before you left England a strange chance led me into the heart of a manufacturing town – a town which was being ravaged by typhus fever; I was in a very weak state of health, and, as might be expected, I caught this fever. I was warned, when it was perhaps not yet too late to have taken precautions which might have saved me, but I would not take these precautions. I was too great a coward to commit suicide. Some people say a man is too brave to kill himself; I was not, but I was too much a coward. Life was hateful, but I was afraid to die. Yet I would not avert a danger which had not been my own seeking: let the fever kill me, if it would. Ellinor, my wish is fast being accomplished. I am dying.'

'Horace, Horace!' She took his wasted hand in hers, and pressed it to her lips.

He drew it away as if he had been stung.

'For God's sake, Ellinor, no tenderness! That I cannot bear. For four years you have never seen me without a mask. I am going to let it fall. Henceforward you will think of me with scorn and detestation.'

'Scorn you, Horace – never!'

He waved his hand impatiently, as if to wave away protestations that must soon be falsified.

'Wait,' he said; 'you do not know.' Then, after a brief pause, he continued, 'Ellinor, I have not been the kindest or the most tender of guardians, have I, to my beautiful young ward? You reproached me with my cold indifference one day soon after your marriage, in the little drawing room in Hertford Street.'

'You remember that?'

'I remember that. Yes, Ellinor. There are few words spoken by your lips which I do not remember, together with the tone in which they were spoken, and the place where I heard them.

I say, I have not been a kind or affectionate guardian – have I, Ellinor?'

'You were so once, Horace,' she said.

'I was so once! When?'

'Before my uncle left me that wretched fortune.'

'That wretched fortune – yes, *that* divided us at once and for ever. Ellinor, there were two reasons for this pitiful comedy of coldness and indifference. Can you guess one of them?'

'No,' she answered.

'You cannot? I affected an indifference I did not feel, or pretended an apathy which was a lie from first to last, because I loved you with the whole strength of my heart and soul, from the first to the last.'

'O, Horace, Horace, for pity's sake!'

She stretched out her hands imploringly, as if she would prevent the utterance of the words which seemed to break her heart.

'Ellinor, when you were seventeen years of age, you had no thought of succeeding to your uncle's property. It would have been, upon the whole, a much more natural thing for him to have left it to his adopted son, Henry Dalton. Your father fully expected that he would do so. I expected the same. Your father entrusted me with the custody of your little income, and I discharged my trust honestly. I was a great speculator; I dabbled with thousands, and cast down heavy sums every day as a gambler throws down a card upon the gaming table; and to me your mother's little fortune was so insignificant a trust that its management never gave me a moment's thought or concern. At this time I was going on in a fair way to become a rich man – in fact, was a rich man; and at this time I was an honourable man. I loved you – loved you as I never believed I could love – my beautiful, innocent ward. How could it well be otherwise? I am not a coxcomb, Ellinor, but I dared to say to myself, "I love, and am beloved again". Those dark-grey eyes had told me the secret of a girl's confiding heart, and I thought myself more than happy, only too deeply blest. O, my darling, my darling, if I had spoken then!'

Mrs Dalton's face was buried in her hands as she knelt by his pillow, and she was sobbing aloud.

'There was time enough, I said. This, Ellinor, was the happiest period of my life. Do you remember our quiet evenings in the rue Saint-Dominique, when I left business and business cares behind me in Verulam buildings, and ran over here to spend a week in my young ward's society? Do you remember the books we read together? Good heavens, there is a page of Lamartine's odes which I can see before me as I speak! I can see the lights and shadows which I taught you to put under the cupola of a church in Munich which you once painted in water-colours. I can recall every thought, every word, every pleasure, and every emotion of that sweet and tranquil time in which I hoped and believed that you, Ellinor, would be my wife.'

She lifted her face, blotted by her tears, looked at him for one brief instant, and then let her head fall again upon her clasped hands.

'Your uncle died, Ellinor, and this airy castle, which I had reared with such confidence, was shattered to the ground. The fortune was left to you on condition that you should marry Henry Dalton. Women are ambitious. You would scarcely resign such a fortune. You would marry young Dalton. This was the lawyer's answer to the all-important question. But those tender grey eyes, looking up shyly from under their dark lashes, had told a sweet secret, and perhaps your generous heart might count this fortune a small thing to cast away for the sake of the man you loved. This was the lover's answer; and I hoped still to win my darling. You were not to be made acquainted with the conditions of your uncle's will until you attained your majority. You were, at the time of his death, not quite twenty years of age; there was therefore an entire year in which you would remain ignorant of the penalties attached to this unexpected wealth. In the mean time I, as sole executor (your uncle, you see, trusted me most entirely), had the custody of the funded property bequeathed to you.'

'I have told you, Ellinor, that I was a speculator. My profession threw me in the way of speculation. Confident in the power of my own intellect, I staked my fortune on the wonderful hazards of the year '46. I doubled that fortune, trebled, quadrupled it, and, when it had grown to be four times its original bulk, I staked it again. It was out of my hands, but it was invested in, as I thought, so safe a speculation, that it was as secure as if it had never been withdrawn from Consols.[7] The railway company of which I was a director was one of the richest and most flourishing in England. My own fortune, as I have told you, was entirely invested, and was doubling itself rapidly. As your uncle's trustee, as your devoted friend, your interests were dearer to me than my own. Why should I not speculate with your fortune, double it, and then say to you, "See, Ellinor, here are two fortunes of which you are mistress; one you owe to Henry Dalton, under the conditions of your uncle's will; the other is yours alone. You are rich. You are free, without any sacrifice, to marry the man you love; and this is my work"? This is what I thought to have said to you at the close of the great year of speculation, 1846.'

'O Horace, Horace, I see it all. Spare yourself, spare me. Do not tell me any more.'

'Spare myself? No, Ellinor, not one pang; I deserve to drain my bitter cup to the dregs. You were right in what you said in the boudoir at Sir Lionel's. The money was not my own; no sophistry, no ingenious twisting of facts and forcing of conclusions, could ever make it mine. How do I know even now that your interest was really my only motive? How do I know that it was not, indeed, the gambler's guilty madness which impelled me to my crime? How do I know – how do I know? Enough, the crash came; my fortune and yours were together engulfed in that vast whirlpool; and I, the trusted friend of your dead father, the conscientious lawyer, whose name had become a synonym for honour and honesty – I Horace Welmoden Margrave, only lineal descendant of the royalist Captain Margrave, who perished at Worcester, fighting for his king and the honour of his noble race – I knew myself to be a cheat and a swindler.'

'No, no, Horace. You were only mistaken.'

'Mistaken, Ellinor! Yes, that is one of the words invented by dishonest men to slur over their dishonesty. The fraudulent banker whose ruin involves the ruin of thousands is, after all, his friends say, only mistaken. The clerk who robs his employer in the insane hope of ultimately restoring what he abstracts is, as his counsel pleads to soft-hearted jurymen with sons of their own, only mistaken. The speculator who plays the great game of commercial hazard with another man's money, he, too, dares to look at the world with a piteous face, and cry, "Alas, I was only mistaken!" No, Ellinor, I have never put in that plea. From the moment of that dreadful crash, which changed hope to despair, and prosperity to desolation, I have at least tried to look my fate in the face. But I have not borne all my own burdens, Ellinor. The weight of my crime has fallen upon the shoulders of Henry Dalton.'

'Henry Dalton, my husband!'

'Yes, Ellinor, your husband, Henry Dalton, the truest and most generous of men.'

'You praise him so much,' she said rather bitterly.

'Yes, Ellinor, I am weak enough and wicked enough to feel a cruel pain in being compelled to do so; it is the one poor reparation I can make him. God knows I have done him injury enough.'

The exertion of talking for so long a time had completely exhausted the dying man, and he fell back, half-fainting, upon the pillows. The sister of charity, summoned from the next apartment by Ellinor, gave him a restorative; and in low tremulous voice he continued,

'From the moment of my ruin, Ellinor, I felt and knew that you were lost to me. I could bear this; I did not think my life would be a long one. *Vogue la galère!*[8] Let it go on its dark way to the end. I say I could bear this, but I could not bear the thought of your contempt, your aversion; that punishment would have been too bitter. I could not come to you, and say, "I love you, I have always loved you; I love you as I never before loved, as I never hoped to love again; but I am a swindler and a cheat, and you can never be mine." No, Ellinor, I could not do this; and the day of your majority was close at hand. Some step must be taken, and the only thing that could save me from your contempt was the generosity of Henry Dalton.

'I had heard a great deal of your uncle's adopted son, and I had met him very often at Arden; I knew him to be as true-hearted a man as ever lived. I determined, therefore, to throw myself upon his generosity, and to reveal all. "He will despise me, but I can bear his contempt better than the scorn of the woman I loved." I said this to myself, and one night – the night after Henry Dalton had first seen you, and had been already won by your grace and beauty – I took him to my chambers in Verulam buildings, and after binding him to secrecy, told him all.

'You now understand the cruel position in which this young man was placed. The fortune, of which he was supposed to become possessor on marrying you, was a thing of the past. You were penniless, except, indeed, for the hundred a year coming to you from your mother's property. His solemn oath forbade him to reveal this to you; and for three years he endured your contempt, and was silent. Judge now of the wrong I have done him. Judge now the noble heart which you have tortured.'

'O Horace, Horace, what misery this money has brought upon us.'

'No, Ellinor. What misery one deviation from the straight road of honour has brought upon us! Ellinor, my dearest, my only beloved, can you forgive the man who has so truly loved, yet so deeply injured you?'

'Forgive you!'

She rose from her knees, and smoothing the ruffled hair from his forehead with tender, pitying hands, looked him full in the face.

'Horace,' she said, 'when, long ago, you thought I loved you, you read my heart aright; but the depth and truth of that love you could never read. Now, now that I am the wife of another, another to whom I owe so very much affection in reparation of the wrong I have done him, I dare tell you without wrong to him, how much I loved you. And you ask me to forgive! As freely as I would have resigned this money for your sake, can I forgive you for the loss of it. This confession has set all right. I will be a good wife to Henry Dalton, and you and he may be sincere friends yet.'

'What, Ellinor, do you think that, did I not know myself to be dying, I could have made this confession? No, you see me now under the influence of stimulants which give me a false strength; of the excitement which is strong enough to master even death. Tomorrow night, Ellinor, the doctors tell me, there will no longer be in this weary world a weak, vacillating, dishonourable wretch called Horace Margrave.'

He stretched out his attenuated hands, drew her towards him, and imprinted one kiss upon her forehead.

'The first and the last, Ellinor,' he said. 'Goodbye.'

His face changed to a deadlier white, and he fell back, fainting. The physician, peeping in at the half-open door, beckoned to Ellinor,

'You must leave him at once, my dear madame,' he said. 'Had I not seen the disturbed state of his mind, I should never have permitted this interview.'

'O monsieur, tell me, can you save him?'

'Only by a miracle, madame; a miracle far beyond medical skill.'

'You yourself, then, have no hope?'

'Alas, no, madame!'

She bowed her head. The physician took her hand in his and pressed it with a fatherly tenderness, looking at her earnestly and mournfully.

'Send for me tomorrow,' she said imploringly.

'I will send you tidings of his state. Adieu!'

She bent her head once more, and, without another word, hurried from the room.

The following morning, as she was seated in her own apartment, she was once more summoned to the drawing room.

The sister of charity was there, talking to her aunt. They both looked grave and thoughtful, and glanced anxiously at Ellinor as she entered the room.

'He is worse?' said Ellinor to the sister, before a word had been spoken.

'Unhappily, yes. Madame, he is –'

'O, do not tell me any more! For pity's sake, for pity's sake!' she exclaimed.

She walked to the window, and stood there, absent and meditative, looking with tearless eyes into the street below, and out at the cheerless grey of the autumn sky.

She was thinking how strange the world looked to her now that Horace Margrave was dead.

They buried Horace Margrave in the cemetery of Père Lachaise. There had been some thoughts of conveying his ashes to his native country, that they might rest in the parish church of Margrave, a little village in Westmoreland, the chancel of which church was decorated with a recumbent statue of Algernon Margrave, cavalier, who fell at Worcester fight; but as the deceased had no nearer relations than a few second cousins in the army and the church, and a superannuated admiral, his great-uncle, and as it was furthermore discovered that the accomplished solicitor of Verulam buildings, Gray's Inn, had left not a penny behind him, the idea was quickly abandoned, and the last remains of the admired Horace were left to decay in a foreign grave.

It was never fully known who caused the simple monument which ultimately adorned his resting place to be erected. It was a plain block of marble; no pompous Latin epitaph, or long list of virtues, was thereon engraved; but a half-burned torch, reversed, was sculptured at the bottom of the tablet, and from the smoke of the expiring torch a butterfly mounted upwards. Above this design were inscribed the name and age of the deceased.

The night following the day of Horace Margrave's funeral, Henry Dalton was seated, hard at work, at his chambers in the Temple.

The light of the office lamp, falling upon his quiet face, revealed a mournful and careworn expression not usual to him.

He looked ten years older since his marriage with Ellinor.

He had fought the battle of life and lost, – lost in that great battle which some hold so lightly, but which to others is an earnest fight, – lost in the endeavour to win his wife he had so tenderly loved.

He had now nothing left to him but his profession, – no other ambition, no other hope.

'I will work hard,' he thought, 'that she, though separated from me for ever, may still derive every joy of those poor joys which money can buy, from my labour.'

He had heard nothing of Horace Margrave's journey to Paris, his illness, or his death. He had no hope of being released from the oath which bound him to silence – to silence which he had sworn to preserve so long as Horace Margrave lived.

Tired, but still persevering, and absorbed in a difficult case which needed all his professional acumen, he read and wrote on, until past eleven o'clock.

Just as the clocks were chiming the half-hour after eleven, the bell of his outer door rang loudly, as if pulled by an agitated hand.

His chambers were on the first floor; on the floor below were those of a gentleman who always left at six o'clock.

'I do not expect anyone at such an hour; but it may be for me,' he thought.

He heard his clerk open the door, and went on writing without once lifting his head.

Three minutes afterwards, the door of his own office suddenly opened, and a person entered unannounced. He looked up suddenly. A lady dressed in mourning, with her face hidden by a thick veil, stood near the door.

'Madame,' he said with some surprise, 'may I ask –'

The late visitor came hurriedly from the door by which she stood, lifted her veil, and fell on her knees at his feet.

'Ellinor!'

'Yes. I am in mourning for Horace Margrave, my unhappy guardian. He died a week ago in Paris. He told me all. Henry, my friend, my husband, my benefactor, can you forgive me?'

Henry Dalton passed his hand rapidly across his eyes, and turned his face away from her.

Presently he raised her in his arms, and drew her to his breast.

'Ellinor,' he cried in a broken voice, 'I have suffered so long and so bitterly that I can scarcely bear this great emotion. My dearest, my ever-beloved wife, are we indeed at last set free from the miserable secret which has blighted our lives? Horace Margrave –'

'Is dead, Henry. I once loved him very dearly. I freely forgave him the injury he did me. Tell me that you forgive him too.'

'From my inmost heart, Ellinor.'

The Mystery at Fernwood

'No, Isabel, I do *not* consider that Lady Adela seconded her son's invitation at all warmly.'

This was the third time within the last hour that my aunt had made the above remark. We were seated opposite each other in a first-class carriage of the York express, and the flat fields of ripening wheat were flitting by us like yellow shadows under the afternoon sunshine. We were going on a visit to Fernwood, a country mansion ten miles from York, in order that I might become acquainted with the family of Mr Lewis Wendale, to whose only son Laurence I was engaged to be married.

Laurence Wendale and I had only been acquainted during the brief May and June of my first London season, which I – orphan heiress of a wealthy Calcutta merchant – had passed under the roof of my aunt, Mrs Maddison Trevor, the dashing widow of a major in the Life Guards, and my father's only sister. Mrs Trevor had made many objections to this brief six weeks' engagement between Laurence and me; but the impetuous young Yorkshireman had overruled everything. What objection could there be? he asked. He was to have two thousand a year and Fernwood at his father's death; forty thousand pounds from a maiden aunt the day he came of age – for he was not yet one-and-twenty, my impetuous lover. As for his family, Mrs Trevor looked into Burke's *County Families* for the Wendales of Fernwood. His mother was Lady Adela, youngest daughter of Lord Kingwood, of Castle Kingwood, County Kildare. What objection could my aunt have, then? His family did not know me, and might not approve of the match, urged my aunt. Laurence laughed aloud; a loud ringing peal of that merry, musical laughter I loved so well to hear.

'Not approve!' he cried – 'not love my little Bella! That is too good a joke!' On which immediately followed an invitation to Fernwood, seconded by a note from Lady Adela Wendale.

To this note my aunt was never tired of taking objection. It was cold, it was constrained; it had been only written to please Laurence. How little I thought of the letter! And yet it was the first faint and shadowy indication of that terrible rock ahead upon which my life was to be wrecked; the first feeble link in the chain of the one great mystery in which the fate of so many was involved.

The letter was cold, certainly. Lady Adela started by declaring she should be most happy to see us; she was all anxiety to be introduced to her charming daughter-in-law. And then my lady ran off to tell us how dull Fernwood was, and how she feared we should regret our long journey into the heart of Yorkshire to a lonely country house, where we should find no one but a captious invalid, a couple of nervous women, and a young man devoted to farming and field sports.

But I was not afraid of being dull where my light-hearted Laurence was; and I overruled all my aunt's objections, ordered half a dozen new dresses, and carried Mrs Maddison Trevor off to the Great Northern Station before she had time to remonstrate.

Laurence had gone on before to see that all was prepared for us; and had promised to meet us at York, and drive us over to Fernwood in his mail phaeton. He was standing on the platform as the train entered the station, radiant with life and happiness.

Laurence Wendale was very handsome; but perhaps his greatest charm consisted in that wonderful vitality, that untiring energy and indomitable spirit, which made him so different from all other young men whom I had met. So great was this vitality, that, by some magnetic influence, it seemed to communicate itself to others. I was never tired when Laurence was with me. I could waltz for longer with him as my partner;

ride longer in the Row with him for my cavalier; sit out an opera or examine an exhibition of pictures with less fatigue when he was near. His presence pervaded a whole house; his joyous laugh ran through every room. It seemed as if where he was sorrow could not come.

I felt this more than ever as we drew nearer Fernwood. The country was bleak and bare; wide wastes of moorland stretched away on either side of the byroad down which we drove. The afternoon sunshine had faded out, leaving a cold grey landscape, and shutting in the dim horizon. But no influence of scenery or atmosphere could affect Laurence. His spirits were higher than usual this afternoon.

'They have fitted up the oak rooms for you, ladies,' he said. 'Such solemn and stately chambers, with high-canopied beds crowned with funeral plumes; black-oak panelling; portraits of dead-and-gone Wendales: Mistress Aurora, with pannier hoops and a shepherdess's crook; Mistress Lydia, with ringlets *à la sevigné* and a pearl necklace; Mortimer Wendale, in a Ramilies wig; Theodore, with lovelocks, velvet doublet, and Spanish-leather boots. Such a collection of them! You may expect to see them all descend from their frames in the witching time of night to warm their icy fingers at your sea coal fires. Your expected arrival has made quite a sensation in our dull old abode. My mother has looked up from the last new novel half a dozen times this day, I verily believe, to ask if all due preparations were being made; while my dear, active, patient, indefatigable sister Lucy has been running about superintending the arrangements ever since breakfast.

'Your sister Lucy!' I said, catching at his last words; 'I shall so love her, Laurence.'

'I hope you will, darling,' he answered, almost gravely, 'for she has been the best and dearest sister to me. And yet I'm half afraid; Lucy is ten years older than you – grave, reserved, sometimes almost melancholy; but if ever there was a banished angel treading this earth in human form, my sister Lucy surely is that guardian spirit.'

'Is she like you, Laurence?'

'Like me! O, no, not in the least. She is only my half-sister you know. She resembles her mother, who died young.'

We were at the gates of Fernwood when he said this, – high wooden gates, with stone pillars moss-grown and dilapidated; a tumbledown looking lodge, kept by a slatternly woman, whose children were at play in a square patch of ground planted with cabbages and currant bushes, fenced in with a rotten paling, and ambitiously called a garden. From this lodge entrance a long avenue stretched away for about half a mile, at the end of which a great red brick mansion, built in the Tudor style, frowned at us, rather as if in defiance than in welcome. The park was entirely uncultivated; the trunks of the trees were choked with the tangled underwood; the fern grew deep in the long vistas, broken here and there by solitary pools of black water, on whose quiet borders we heard the flap of the heron's wing, and the dull croaking of an army of frogs.

Lady Adela was right. Fernwood *was* a dull place. I could scarcely repress a shudder as we drove along the dark avenue, while my poor aunt's teeth chattered audibly. Accustomed to spend three parts of the year in Onslow square, and the autumn months at Brighton or Ryde, this dreary Yorkshire mansion was a terrible trial to her rather over-sensitive nerves.

Laurence seemed to divine the reason for our silence. 'The place is frightfully neglected, Mrs Trevor,' he said apologetically; 'but I do not mean this sort of thing to last, I assure you. Before I bring my delicate little Bella to reign at Fernwood, I shall have landscape gardeners and upholsterers by the score, and do my best to convert this dreary wilderness into a terrestrial paradise. I cannot tell you why the place has been suffered to fall into decay; certainly not for want of money, still less for want of opportunity, for my father is an idle man, to whom one would imagine restoring and rebuilding would afford a delightful hobby. No, there is no reason why the place should have been so neglected.'

He said this more to himself than to us, as if the words were spoken in answer to some long train of thought of his own. I watched his face earnestly, for I had seldom seen him look so thoughtful. Presently he said, with more of his usual manner,

'As you are close upon the threshold of Fernwood now, ladies, I ought perhaps to tell you that you will find ours a most low-spirited family. With everything in life to make us happy, we seem for ever under a cloud. Ever since I can remember my poor father, he has been sinking slowly into decay, almost in the same way as this neglected place, till now he is a confirmed invalid, without any positive illness. My mother reads novels all day, and seems to exist upon sal volatile and spirits of lavender. My sister, the only active person in the house, is always thoughtful, and very often melancholy. Mind, I merely tell you this to prepare you for anything you may see; not to depress you, for you may depend upon my exertions towards reforming this dreary household, which has sunk into habitual despondency from sheer easy fortune and want of exertion.'

The phaeton drew up before a broad flight of stone steps as Laurence ceased speaking, and in five minutes more he had assisted my aunt and myself to alight, and had ushered us into the presence of Lady Adela and Miss Lucy Wendale.

We found Lady Adela, as her son's description had given us reason to expect, absorbed in a novel. She threw down her book as we entered, and advanced to meet us with considerable cordiality; rather, indeed, as if she really were grateful to us for breaking in upon her solitary life.

'It is so good of you to come,' she said folding me in her slender arms with an almost maternal embrace, 'and so kind of you too, my dear Mrs Trevor, to abandon all your town pleasures for the sake of bringing this dear girl to me. Believe me, we will do all in our power to make you comfortable, if you can put up with very limited society; for we have received no company whatever since my son's childhood, and I do not think my visiting list could muster half a dozen names.'

Lady Adela was an elegant looking woman, in the very prime of her life; but her handsome face was thin and care-worn, and premature wrinkles gathered about her melancholy blue eyes and thoughtful mouth. While she was talking to my aunt, Lucy Wendale and I drew nearer to each other.

Laurence's half-sister was by no means handsome; pale and sallow, with dark hair and rather dull grey eyes, she looked as if some hidden sorrow had quenched out the light of her life long ago, in her earliest youth; some sorrow that had neither been forgotten, nor lessened by time, but that had grown with her growth, and strengthened with her strength, until it had become part of her very self, – some disappointed attachment, I thought, some cruel blow that had shattered a girl's first dream, and left a broken-hearted woman to mourn the fatal delusion. In my utter ignorance of life, I thought these were the only griefs which ever left a woman's life desolate.

'You will try and be happy at Fernwood, Isabel,' Miss Wendale said gently, as she drew me into a seat by her side, while Laurence bent fondly over us both. I do not believe, dear as we were to each other, that my Laurence ever loved me as he loved this pale-faced half-sister. 'You will try and be happy, will you not, dear Isabel? Laurence has been breaking in the prettiest chestnut mare in all Yorkshire, I think, that you may explore the country with us. I have heard what a daring horsewoman you are. The pianos have been put in tune for you, and the billiard table re-covered, that you may have exercise on rainy days; and if we cannot give you much society, we will do all else to prevent your feeling dull.'

'I shall be very happy here with you, dear Lucy,' I said; 'but you tell me so much of the dullness of Fernwood, while, I daresay, you yourself must have a hundred associations that make the old places very dear to you.'

She looked down as I spoke, and a very faint blush broke through the sallow paleness of her complexion.

'I am not very fond of Fernwood,' she said gravely.

It was at Fernwood, then, that the great sorrow of her life came upon her, I thought.

'No, Lucy,' said Laurence impatiently, 'everybody knows this dull place is killing you by inches, and yet nothing on earth can induce you to quit it. When we all go to Scarborough or Burlington, when mamma goes to Harrogate, when I run up to town to rub off my provincial rust, and see what the world is really made of outside these dreary gates, – you obstinately persist in staying at home; and the only reasons you can urge for doing so is, that you must remain here to take care of that unfortunate invalid of yours, Mr William.'

I was holding Lucy's hand in mine, and I felt the poor wasted little fingers tremble as her brother spoke. My curiosity was strongly aroused.

'Mr William!' I exclaimed half involuntarily.

'Ah, to be sure, Bella, I forgot to tell you of that member of our household, but as I have never seen him, I may be forgiven the omission. This Mr William is a poor relative of my father's; a hopeless invalid, bedridden, I believe – is he not, Lucy? –

who requires a strong man and an experienced nurse to look after him, and who occupies the entire upper story of one wing of the house. Poor Mr William, invalid as he is, must certainly be a most fascinating person. My mother goes to see him every day, but as stealthily as if she were paying a secret visit to some condemned criminal. I have often met my father coming away from his rooms, pale and melancholy; and, as for my sister Lucy, she is so attached to this sick dependant of ours, that, as I have just said, nothing will induce her to leave the house, for fear his nurse or his valet should fail in their care of him.'

I still held Lucy's hand, but it was perfectly steady now. Could this poor relative, this invalid dependant, have any part in the sorrowful mystery that had overshadowed her life? And yet, no; I thought that could scarcely be, for she looked up with such perfect self-possession as she answered her brother:

'My whole life has gradually fallen into the duty of attendance upon this poor young man, Laurence; and I will never leave Fernwood while he lives.'

A young man! Mr William was a young man, then.

Lucy herself led us to the handsome suite of apartments prepared for my aunt and me. My aunt's room was separated from mine by a corridor, out of which opened two dressing rooms and a pretty little boudoir, all looking on to the park. My room was at the extreme angle of the building; it had two doors, one leading to the corridor communicating with my aunt's apartments, the other opening into a gallery running the entire length of the house. Looking out into this gallery, I saw that the opposite wing was shut in by a baize door. It was most likely the barrier which closed the outer world upon Laurence Wendale's invalid relation.

Lucy left us as soon as we were installed in our apartments. While I was dressing for dinner, the housekeeper, a stout, elderly woman, came to ask me if I found everything I required.

'As you haven't brought your own servant with you, miss,' she said, 'Miss Lucy told me to place her maid Sarah entirely at your service. Miss gives very little work to a maid herself, so Sarah has plenty of leisure time on her hands, and you'll find her a very respectable young woman.'

I told her that I could do all I wanted for myself; but before she left me I could not resist asking her one question about the mysterious invalid.

'Are Mr William's rooms at this end of the house?' I asked.

The woman looked at me with an almost scared expression, and was silent for a moment.

'Has Mr Laurence been saying anything to you about Mr William?' she said, rather anxiously as I thought.

'Mr Laurence and his sister Miss Lucy were both talking of him just now.'

'O, indeed, miss,' answered the woman with an air of relief; 'the poor gentleman's rooms are at the other end of the gallery, miss.'

'Has he lived here long?' I asked.

'Nigh upon twenty years, miss – above twenty years, I'm thinking.'

'I suppose he is distantly related to the family.'

'Yes, miss.'

'And quite dependent on Mr Wendale?'

'Yes, miss.'

'It is very good of your master to have supported him for so many years, and to keep him in such comfort.'

'My master is a very good man, miss.'

The woman seemed determined to give me as little information as possible; but I could not resist one more question.

'How is it that in all these years Mr Laurence has never seen this invalid relation?' I asked.

It seemed that this question, of all others, was the most embarrassing to the housekeeper. She turned first red and then pale, and said, in a very confused manner, 'The poor gentleman never leaves his room, miss; and Mr Laurence has such high spirits, bless his dear heart, and has such a noisy, rackety way with him, that he's no fit company for an invalid.'

It was evidently useless trying for further information, so I abandoned the attempt, and bidding the housekeeper good afternoon, began to dress my hair before the massive oak-framed looking glass.

'The truth of the matter is,' I said to myself, 'that after all there is nothing more to be said about it. I have tried to create a mystery out of the simplest possible family arrangement. Mr Wendale has a bed-ridden relative, too poor and too help-less to support himself. What more natural that that he should give him house room in this dreary old mansion, where there seems to be space enough to lodge a regiment?'

I found the family assembled in the drawing room. Mr Wendale was the wreck of a very handsome man. He must in early life have resembled Laurence; but, as my lover had said, it seemed as if he and the house and grounds of Fernwood had fallen into decay together. But notwithstanding his weak state of health, he gave us a warm welcome, and did the honours of his hospitable dinner table with the easy grace of a gentleman.

After dinner, my aunt and Lady Adela sat at one end of the windows talking; while Laurence, Lucy, and I loitered upon a long stone terrace outside the drawing room, watching the last low crimson streak of the August sunset fade behind the black trunks of the trees, and melt away into faint red splashes upon the water pools amongst the brushwoods. We were very happy together; Laurence and I talking of a hundred different subjects – telling Lucy our London adventures, describing our fashionable friends, our drives and rides, fêtes, balls, and dinners; she, with a grave smile upon her lips, listening to us with an almost maternal patience.

'I must take you over the old house tomorrow, Isabel,' Laurence said in the course of the evening. 'I suppose Lucy did not tell you that she had put you into the haunted room?'

'No, indeed!'

'You must not listen to this silly boy, my dear Isabel,' said Miss Wendale. 'Of course, like all other old houses, Fernwood can boast its ghost story; but since no one in my father's life-time has ever seen a phantom, you may imagine that it is not a very formidable one.'

'But you own there *is* a ghost!' I exclaimed eagerly. 'Pray tell me the story.'

'I'll tell you, Bella,' answered Laurence, 'and then you'll know what sort of a visitor to expect when the bells of Fernwood church, hidden away behind the elms yonder, tremble on the stroke of midnight. A certain Sir Humphrey Wendale, who lived in the time of Henry the Eighth, was wronged by his wife, a very beautiful woman. Had he acted according to the ordinary fashion of the time, he would have murdered the lady and his rival; but our ancestor was of a more original turn of mind, and he hit upon an original plan of vengeance. He turned every servant out of Fernwood House; and one morning, when the unhappy lady was sleeping, he locked every door of the mansion, secured every outlet and inlet, and rode away merrily in the summer sunshine, leaving his wife to die of hunger. Fernwood is lonely enough even now, heaven knows! But it was lonelier in those distant days. A passing traveller may now and then have glanced upward at the smokeless chimneys, dimly visible across the trees, as he rode under the park palings; but none ever dreamed that the deserted mansion had one luckless tenant. Fifteen months afterwards, when Sir Humphrey rode home from foreign travel, he had some difficulty in forcing the door of the chamber in which you are to sleep: the withered and skeleton form of his dead wife had fallen across the threshold.'

'What a horrible story!' I exclaimed with a shiver.

'It is only a legend, dear Isabel,' said Lucy; 'like all tradition, exaggerated and distorted into due proportions of poetic horror. Pray do not suffer your mind to dwell upon such a fable.'

'Indeed I hope it is not true,' I answered. 'How fond people are of linking mysteries and horrors such as this with the history of an old family! And yet we never fall across any such family mystery in our own days.'

I slept soundly that night at Fernwood, undisturbed by the attenuated shadow of Sibyl Wendale, Sir Humphrey's unhappy wife. The bright sunshine was reflected in the oak panels of my room, and the larks were singing aloft in a cloudless blue sky, when I awoke. I found my aunt quite reconciled to her visit.

'Lady Adela is a very agreeable woman,' she said; 'quiet, perhaps, to a fault, but with that high-bred tone which is always charming. Lucy Wendale seems a dear good girl, though evidently a confirmed old maid. You will find her of inestimable use when you are married – that is to say, if you ever have to manage this great rambling place, which will of course fall to your lot in the event of poor Mr Wendale's death.'

As for myself, I was as happy at Fernwood as the August days were long. Lucy Wendale rode remarkably well. It was the only amusement for which she cared; and she and her horses were on terms of the most devoted attachment. Laurence, his sister, and I were therefore constantly out together, riding amongst the hills about Fernwood, and exploring the country for twenty miles round.

Indoors, Lucy left us very much to ourselves. She was the ruling spirit in the house, and but for her everything must have fallen utterly to decay. Lady Adela read novels, or made a feeble attempt at amusing my aunt with her conversation. Mr Wendale kept his room until dinner; while Laurence and I played, sang, sketched, and rattled the billiard balls over the green cloth whenever the bad weather drove us to indoor amusements.

One day, while sketching the castellated facade of the old mansion, I noticed a peculiar circumstance connected with the suite of rooms occupied by the invalid, Mr William. These rooms were at the extreme left angle of the building, and were lighted by a range of six windows. I was surprised by observing that every one of these windows was of ground glass. I asked Laurence the reason of this.

'Why, I believe the glare of light was too much for Mr William,' he answered, 'so my father, who is the kindest creature in Christendom, had the windows made opaque, as you see them now.'

'Has the alteration been long made?'

'It was made when I was about six years old; I have rather a vague recollection of the event, and I should not perhaps remember it but for one circumstance. I was riding about down here one morning on my Shetland pony, when my attention was attracted by a child who was looking through one of those windows. I was not old enough to see his face, but I do fancy he must have been about my own age. He beckoned to me, and I was riding across the grass to respond to his invitation, when my sister Lucy appeared at the window and snatched the child away. I suppose he was someone belonging to the female attendant upon Mr William, and had strayed unnoticed into the invalid's rooms. I never saw him again; and the next day a glazier came over from York, and made the alteration in the windows.'

'But Mr William must have air; I suppose the windows are sometimes opened,' I said.

'Never, they are each ventilated by a single pane, which, if you observe, is open now.'

'I cannot help pitying this poor man,' I said, after a pause, 'shut out almost from the light of heaven by his infirmities, and deprived of all society.'

'Not entirely so,' answered Laurence. 'No one knows how many stolen hours my sister Lucy devotes to her poor invalid.'

'Perhaps he is a very studious man, and finds his consolation in literary or scientific pursuits,' I said; 'does he read very much?'

'I think not. I never heard of his having any books got for him.'

'But one thing has puzzled me, Laurence,' I continued. 'Lucy spoke of him the other day as a young man, and yet Mrs Porson, your housekeeper, told me he had lived at Fernwood for upwards of twenty years.'

'As for that,' answered Laurence carelessly, 'Lucy no doubt remembers him as a young man upon his first arrival here, and continues to call him so from mere force of habit. But, pray, my little inquisitive Bella, do not rack your brains about this poor relation of ours. To tell the truth, I have become so used to his unseen presence in the house, that I have ceased to think of him at all. I meet a grim woman, dressed in black merino, coming out of the green baize door, and I know that she is Mr William's nurse; or I see a solemn-faced man, and I am equally assured that he is Mr William's servant, James Beck, who has grown grey in his office; I encounter his doctor riding away from Fernwood on his brown cob, and feel convinced that he has just looked in to see how Mr William is going on; if I miss my sister for an hour in the twilight, I know that she is in the west wing talking to Mr William; but as nobody ever calls upon me to do anything for this poor man, I think no more of the matter.'

I felt these words almost a reproof to what might have appeared idle, or even impertinent, curiosity on my part. And yet the careless indifference of Laurence's manner seemed to jar upon my senses. Could it be that this glad and high-hearted being, whom I so tenderly loved, was selfish – heedless of the sufferings of others? No, it was surely not this that prompted his thoughtless words. It is a positive impossibility for one whose whole nature is life and motion, animation and vigour, to comprehend for one brief moment the horror of the invalid's darkened rooms and solitary days.

I had been nearly a month at Fernwood, when, for the first time during our visit, Laurence left us. One of his old schoolfellows, a lieutenant in the army, was quartered with his regiment at York, and Laurence had promised to dine with the mess. Though I had been most earnest in requesting him to accept the invitation, I could not help feeling dull and dispirited as I watched him drive away down the avenue, and felt that for the first time we were to spend the long autumn evening without him. Do what I would, the time hung heavily on my hands. The September sunset was beautiful, and Lucy and I walked up and down the terrace after dinner, while Mr Wendale slept in his easy chair, and my aunt and Lady Adela exchanged drowsy monosyllabic sentences on a couch near the fire, which was always lighted in the evening.

It was in vain that I tried to listen to Lucy's conversation. My thoughts wandered in spite of myself, – sometimes to Laurence in the brilliantly-lit mess room, enlivening a circle of blasé officers with his boisterous gaiety; sometimes, as if in contrast to this, to the dark west room in which the invalid counted the long hours; sometimes to that dim future in whose shadowy years death was to claim our weary host, and Laurence and I were to be master and mistress of Fernwood. I had often tried to picture the place as it would be when it fell into Laurence's hands, and the architects and landscape gardeners came to work their wondrous transformations; but, do what I could, I could never imagine it otherwise than it was, – with straggling ivy hanging forlornly about the moss-stained walls, and solitary pools of stagnant water hiding amongst the tangle brushwood.

Laurence and I were to be married the following spring. He would come of age in February, and I should be twenty in March, – only a year and a month between our ages, and both a great deal too young to marry, my aunt said. After tea, Lucy and I sang and played. Dreary music it seemed to me that night. I thought my voice and the piano were both out of tune, and I left Lucy very rudely in the middle of our favourite duet. I took up twenty books from the crowded drawing room table, only to throw them when I looked into them that night; never had my aunt's conversation sounded so tiresome. I looked from my watch to the old-fashioned timepiece upon the chimney half a dozen times, to find at last that it was scarcely ten o'clock. Laurence had promised to be home by eleven, and had begged Lucy and me to sit up for him.

Eleven struck at last, but Laurence had not kept his promise. My aunt and Lady Adela rose to light their candles. Mr Wendale always retired a little after nine. I pleaded for half an hour longer, and Lucy was too kind not to comply readily.

'Isabel is right,' she said; 'Laurence is a spoilt boy, you know, mamma, and will feel himself very much ill-used if he finds no one up to hear his description of the mess dinner.'

'Only half an hour, then, mind young ladies,' said my aunt. 'I cannot allow you to spoil your complexions on account of dissipated people who drive ten miles to a military dinner. One half-hour; not a moment more, or I shall come down again to scold you both.'

We promised obedience, and my aunt left us. Lucy and I seated ourselves on each side of the low fire, which had burned dull and hollow. I was too much dispirited to talk, and I sat listening to the ticking of the clock, and the occasional falling of a cinder in the bright steel fender. Then that thought came to me which comes to all watchers: what if anything had happened to Laurence? I went to one of the windows, and pulled back the heavy shutters. It was a lovely night; clear, though not moonlit, and myriads of stars gleamed in the cloudless sky. I stood at the window for some time, listening for the wheels and watching for the lamps of the phaeton.

I too was a spoilt child; life had for me been bright and smooth, and the least thought of grief or danger to those that I loved filled me with a wild panic. I turned suddenly round to Lucy, and cried out, 'Lucy, Lucy, I am getting frightened! Suppose anything should have happened to Laurence; those horses are wild and unmanageable sometimes. If he has taken a few glasses of wine – if he trusted the groom to drive – if –'

She came over to me, and took me in her arms as if I had been indeed a little child.

'My darling,' she said, 'my darling Isabel, you must not distress yourself by such fancies as these. He is only half an hour later than he said; and as for danger, dearest, he is beneath the shelter of Providence, without whose safeguard those we love are never secure even for a moment.'

Her quiet manner calmed my agitation. I left the window, and returned shivering to the expiring fire.

'It is nearly three-quarters of an hour now, Bella dear,' she said presently; 'we must keep our promise; and as for Laurence, you will hear the phaeton drive in before you go to sleep, I daresay.'

'I shall not go to sleep until I do hear it,' I answered, as I took my candle and bade her goodnight.

I could not help listening for the welcome sound of the carriage wheels as I crossed the hall and went upstairs. I stopped in the corridor to look into my aunt's room; but she was fast asleep, and I closed the door as softly as I had opened it. It was as I left this room that, glancing down the corridor, I was surprised to see that there was a light in my own bed-chamber. I was prepared to find a fire there, but the light shining through the half-open door was something brighter than the red glow of a fire. I had joined Laurence in laughing at the ghost story; but my first thought on seeing this light was of the shadow of the wretched Lady Sibyl. What if I found her crouching over my hearth!

I was half inclined to go back to my aunt's room, awaken her, and tell her my fears; but one moment's reflection made me ashamed of my cowardice. I went on, and pushed open the door of my room: there was no pale phantom shivering over the open hearth. There was an old-fashioned silver candlestick upon the table, and Laurence, my lover, was seated by the blazing fire; not dressed in the evening costume he had worn for the dinner party, but wrapped in a loose grey woollen dressing gown, and wearing a black-velvet smoking cap upon his chestnut hair.

Without stopping to think of the strangeness of his appearance in my room; without wondering at the fact of his having entered the house unknown either to Lucy or myself; without one thought but joy and relief of mind at seeing him once more, – I ran forward to him, crying out, 'Laurence, Laurence, I am so glad you have come back!'

He – Laurence, my lover, as I thought – the man, the horrible shadow – rose from his chair, snatched up some papers that lay loosely on the table by his side, crumpled them into a ball with one fierce gesture of his strong hand, and flung them at my feet; then, with a harsh dissonant laugh that seemed a mocking echo of the joyous music I loved so well, he stalked out of the door opening on the gallery. I tried to scream, but my dry lips and throat could form no sound. The oak panelling of the room spun round, the walls and ceiling contracted, as if they had been crushing in upon me to destroy me. I fell heavily to the floor; but as I fell I heard the phaeton wheels upon the carriage drive below, and Laurence Wendale's voice calling to the servants.

I can remember little more that happened upon that horrible night. I have a vague recollection of opening my eyes upon a million dazzling lights, which slowly resolved themselves into the one candle held by Lucy Wendale's hand, as she stood beside the bed upon which I was lying. My aunt, wrapped in her dressing gown, sat by my pillow. My face and hair dripped with the vinegar and water they had thrown over me, and I could hear Laurence, in the corridor outside my bedroom door, asking again and again, 'Is she better? Is she quite herself again?'

But of all this I was only dimly conscious; a load of iron seemed pressing upon my forehead, and icy hands seemed riveted upon the back of my head, holding it tightly to the pillow on which it lay. I could no more have lifted it than I could have lifted a ton weight. I could only lie staring with stupid dull eyes at Lucy's pale face, silently wishing that she and my aunt would go away, and leave me to myself.

I suppose I was feverish and a little light-headed all that night, acting over and over again the brief scene of my meeting with the weird shadow of my lover. I had seen the phantom of the man I loved, the horrible duplicate image of that familiar figure, shaped perhaps out of impalpable air, but as terribly distinct to the eye as if it had been a form of flesh and blood.

Lucy was sitting by my bedside when I awoke from a short sleep which had succeeded the long night of fever. How intensely refreshing that brief but deep slumber was to me! How delicious the gradual fading-out of the sense of horror and bewilderment, with all the hideous confusions of delirium, into the blank tranquillity of dreamless sleep! When I awoke my head was still painful, and my frame as feeble as if I had lain for a week on a sick bed; but my brain was cleared, and I was able to think quietly of what had happened.

'Lucy,' I said, 'you do not know what frightened me, or why I fainted.'

'No, dearest, not exactly.'

'But you can know nothing of it, Lucy. You were not with me when I came into this room last night. You did not see –'

I paused, unable to finish my sentence.

'Did not seem whom – or what, dear Isabel?'

'The shadow of your brother Laurence.'

My whole frame trembled with the recollection of my terror of the night before, as I said this; yet I was able to observe

Lucy's face, and I saw that its natural hue had faded to an ashen pallor.

'The shadow, Isabel!' she faltered; not as if in any surprise at my words, but rather as if she merely spoke because she felt obliged to make some reply to me.

'Yes, Lucy,' I said, raising myself upon the pillow, and grasping her wrist, 'the shadow of your brother Laurence. The living, breathing, moving image of your brother, with every lineament and every shade of colouring reflected in the phantom face as they would be reflected in a mirror. Not shadowy, transparent, or vanishing, but as distinct as you are to me at this very moment. Good heavens! Lucy, I give you my solemn word that I heard the phantom footsteps along that gallery as distinctly as I have ever heard the steps of Laurence himself; the firm heavy tread of a strong man.'

Lucy Wendale sat for some time perfectly silent, looking straight before her, – not at me, but out of the half-open window, round which the ivy leaves were fluttering, to the dim moorland melting into purple distance above the treetops in the park. Her profile was turned towards me; but I could see by her firmly-compressed lips and fixed eyes that she was thinking deeply.

Presently she said, slowly and deliberately, without once looking at me as she spoke, 'You must be fully aware, my dearest Isabel, that these delusions are of common occurrence with people of an extremely sensitive temperament. You may be one of those delicately organised persons; you had thrown yourself into a very nervous and hysterical state in your morbid anxiety about Laurence. With your whole mind full of his image, and tormented by all kinds of shadowy terrors about danger to him, what more likely that that you should conjure up an object such as that which you fancy you saw last night?'

'But so palpable, Lucy, so distinct!'

'It would be easy for the brain to shape a distinct as an indistinct form. Grant the possibility of optical delusion, a fact established by a host of witnesses, – and you cannot limit the character of the delusion. But I must get our doctor, Mr Arden, to talk to you about this. He is something of a metaphysician as well as a medical man, and you will be able to cure your mental ills and regulate this feverish pulse of yours at the same time. Laurence has ridden over to York to fetch him, and I daresay they will both be here directly.'

'Lucy, remember you must never tell Laurence the cause of my last night's fainting fit.'

'I never shall, dear. I was about to make the very same request to you. It is much better that he should not know it.'

'Much better; for O, Lucy, do you remember that in all ghost stories the appearance of the shadow, or double, of a living person is a presage of death to that person? The thought of this brings back all my terror. My Laurence, my darling, if anything should happen to him!'

'Come, Bella, Mr Arden must talk to you. In the meantime, here comes Mrs Porson with your breakfast. While you are taking it, I will go to the library, and look for Sir Walter Scott's *Demonology*. You will find several instances in that book of the optical delusions I have spoken of.'

The housekeeper came bustling into the room with a breakfast tray, which she placed on a table by the bed. When she had arranged everything for my comfort, and propped me up with a luxurious pile of pillows, she turned round to speak to Lucy.

'O, Miss Lucy,' she said, 'poor Beck is so awfully cut up. If you'd only just see him, and tell him –'

Lucy silenced her with one look; a brief but all-expressive glance of warning and reproval. I could not help wondering what possible reason there could be for making a mystery of some little trouble of James Beck's.

Mr Arden, the York surgeon, was the most delightful of men. He came with Lucy into my room, and laughed and chatted me out of my low spirits before he had been with me a quarter of an hour. He talked so much of hysteria, optical delusions, false impressions of outward objects, abnormal conditions of the organ of sight, and other semi-mental, semi-physical infirmities, that he fairly bewildered me into agreeing with and believing all he said.

'I hear that you are a most accomplished horsewoman, Miss Morley,' he said, as he rose to leave us; 'and as the day promises to be fine I most strongly recommend a canter across the moors, with Mr Wendale as your cavalier. Go to sleep between this and luncheon; rise in time to eat a mutton chop and drink a glass of bitter ale; ride for two hours in the sunniest part of the afternoon; take a light dinner, and go to bed early; and I will answer for your seeing no more of the ghost. You have no idea how much indigestion had to do with these things. I daresay if I were to see your bill of fare for yesterday I should discover that Lady Adela's cook is responsible for the phantom, and that he made his first appearance among the entrées. Who can wonder that the Germans are a ghost-seeing people, when it is remembered that they eat raspberry jam with roast veal?'

I followed the doctor's advice to the letter; and at three o'clock in the afternoon Laurence and I were galloping across the moorland, tinged with a yellow hazy light in the September sunshine. Like most impressionable people, I soon recovered from my nervous shock; and by the time I sprang from the saddle before the wide stone portico at Fernwood I had almost forgotten my terrors of the previous night.

A fortnight after this my aunt and I left Yorkshire for Brighton, whither Laurence speedily followed us. Before leaving I did all in my power to induce Lucy to accompany us, but in vain. She thanked my aunt for her cordial invitation, but declared that she could not leave Fernwood. We departed, therefore, without having won her, as I had hoped to have done, from the monotony of her solitary life; and without having seen Mr Wendale's invalid dependant, the mysterious occupant of the west wing.

Early in November Laurence was summoned from Brighton by the arrival of a black-bordered letter, written by Lucy, and telling him of his father's death. Mr Wendale had been found by his servant, seated in an easy chair in his study, with his head lying back upon the cushions, and an open book on the carpet at his feet, dead. He had long suffered from disease of the heart.

My lover wrote me long letters from Yorkshire, telling me how his mother and sister bore the blow which had fallen upon them so suddenly. It was a quiet and subdued sorrow rather than a tempestuous grief, which reigned in the narrow circle at Fernwood. Mr Wendale had been an invalid for many years, giving very little of his society to his wife and daughter. His death, therefore, though sudden, had not been unexpected, nor did his loss leave any great blank in that quiet home. Laurence spent Christmas at Fernwood, but returned to us for the New Year; and it was settled that we should go down to Yorkshire early in February, in order to superintend the restoration and alteration of the old place.

All was arranged for our journey, when, on the very day on which we were to start, Laurence came to Onslow square with a letter from his mother, which he had only just received. Lady Adela wrote a few hurried lines to beg us to delay our visit for some days, as they had decided on removing Mr William, before the alterations were commenced, to a cottage which was being prepared for him near York. His patron's death did not leave the invalid dependent on the bounty of Laurence or Lady Adela. Mr Wendale had bequeathed a small estate, worth three hundred a year, in trust for the sole use and benefit of this Mr William Wendale.

Neither Laurence nor I understood why the money should have been left in trust rather than unconditionally to the man himself. But neither he nor I felt deeply interested in the subject; and Laurence was far too careless of business matters to pry into the details of his succession. He knew himself to be the owner of Fernwood and of a handsome income, and that was all he cared to know.

'I will not hear of this visit being delayed an hour,' Laurence said impatiently, as he thrust Lady Adela's crumpled letter into his pocket. 'My poor foolish mother and sister are really too absurd about this first or fifth cousin of ours, William Wendale. Let him leave Fernwood, or let him stay at Fernwood, just as he or his nurse or his medical man may please; but I certainly shall not allow his arrangements to interfere with ours. So, ladies, I shall be perfectly ready to escort you by the eleven o'clock express.'

Mrs Trevor remonstrated, declaring that she would rather delay our visit according to Lady Adela's wish; but my impetuous Laurence would not hear a word, and under a black and moonless February sky we drove up the avenue at Fernwood.

We met Mr Arden in the hall as we entered. There seemed something ominous in receiving our first greeting from the family doctor; and Laurence was for a moment alarmed by his presence.

'My mother – Lucy!' he said anxiously; 'they are well, I hope?'

'Perfectly well. I have not been attending them; I have just come from Mr William.'

'Is he worse?'

'I fear he is rather worse than usual.'

Our welcome was scarcely a cordial one, for both Lucy and Lady Adela were evidently embarrassed by our unexpected arrival. Their black dresses half-covered with crape, the mourning liveries of the servants, the vacant seat of the master, the dismal winter weather, and ceaseless beating of the rain upon the window panes, gave a more than usually dreary aspect to the place, and seemed to chill us to the very soul.

Those who at any period of their lives have suffered some terrible and crushing affliction, some never to be forgotten trouble, for which even the hand of time has no lessening influence, which increases rather than diminishes as the slow course of life carries us farther from it, so that as we look back we do not ask ourselves why the trial seemed so bitter, but wonder rather how we endured even as we did, – those only who have sunk under such a grief as this can know how difficult it is to dissociate the period preceding the anguish from the hour in which it came. I say this lest I should be influenced by after-feelings when I describe the dismal shadows that seemed to brood over the hearth round which Lady Adela, my aunt, Laurence, and myself gathered upon the night of our return to Fernwood.

Lucy had left us; and when her brother inquired about her, Lady Adela said she was with Mr William.

As usual, Laurence chafed at the answer. It was hard, he said, that his sister should have to act as sick-nurse to this man.

'James Beck has gone to York to prepare for William,' answered Lady Adela, 'and the poor boy has no one with him but his nurse.'

The poor boy! I wondered why it was that Lady Adela and her stepdaughter always alluded to Mr William as a young man.

Early next morning, Laurence insisted upon our accompanying him on a circuit of the house, to discuss the intended alterations. I have already described the gallery, running the whole length of the building, at one end of which was situated the suite of rooms occupied by Mr William, and at the other extremity those devoted to Aunt Trevor and myself. Lady Adela's apartments were nearest to those of the invalid, Lucy's next, then the billiard room, and opening out of that the bed and dressing room occupied by Laurence. On the other side of the gallery were servants' and visitors' rooms, and a pretty boudoir sacred to Lady Adela.

Laurence was in very high spirits, planning alterations here and renovations there – bay windows to be thrown out in one direction, and folding doors knocked through in another – till we laughed heartily at him on finding that the pencil memorandum he was preparing for the architect resolved itself into an order for knocking down the old house and building a new one. We had explored every nook and corner in the place, with the one exception of those mysterious apartments in the left wing. Laurence Wendale paused before the green baize door, but after a moment's hesitation tapped for admittance.

'I have never seen Mr William, and it is rather awkward to have to ask to look at his rooms while he is in them; but the necessity of the case will be my excuse for intruding on him. The architect will be here tomorrow, and I want to have all my plans ready to submit to him.'

The baize door was opened by Lucy Wendale; she started at seeing us.

'What do you want, Laurence?' she said.

'To see Mr William's rooms. I shall not disturb him, if he will kindly allow me to glance around his apartments.'

I could see that there was an inner half-glass door behind that in which Lucy was standing.

'You cannot possibly see the rooms today, Laurence,' she said hurriedly. 'Mr William leaves tomorrow morning.'

She came out into the gallery, closing the baize door behind her; but as the shutting of the door reverberated through the gallery, I heard another sound that turned my blood to ice, and made me cling convulsively to Laurence's arms.

The laugh, the same dissonant laugh that I had heard from the spectral lips of my lover's shadow!

'Lucy,' I said, 'did you hear that?'

'What?'

'The laugh, the laugh I heard the night that –'

Laurence had thrown his arm round me, alarmed by my terror. His sister was standing a little way behind him; she put her finger to her lips, looking at me significantly.

'You must be mistaken, Isabel,' she said quietly.

There was some mystery, then, connected with this Mr William – a mystery which for some especial reason was to be concealed from Laurence.

Half an hour after this, Lucy Wendale came to me as I was searching for a book in the library.

'Isabel,' she said, 'I wish to say a few words to you.'

'Yes, dear Lucy.'

'You are to be my sister, and I have perhaps done wrong in concealing from you the one unhappy secret which has clouded the lives of my poor father, my stepmother, and myself.

But long ago, when Laurence was a child, it was deemed expedient that the grief which was so heavy a load for us should, if possible, be spared to him. My father was so passionately devoted to his handsome light-hearted boy that he shrank day by day from the thought of revealing to him the afflicting secret which was such a source of grief to himself. We found that, by constant care and watchfulness, it was possible to conceal all from Laurence, and up to this hour we have done so. But it is perhaps better that you should know all; for you will be able to aid us in keeping the knowledge from Laurence; or, if absolutely necessary, you may by and by break it to him gently, and reconcile him to an irremediable affliction.'

'But this secret – this affliction – it concerns your invalid relation, Mr William?'

'It does, Isabel.'

I know that the words which were to reveal all were trembling upon her lips, – that in one brief moment she would have spoken, and I should have known all. I should have known – in time; but before she could utter a syllable the door was opened by one of the women servants.

'O miss, if you please,' she said, 'Mrs Peters says would you step upstairs this minute?'

Mrs Peters was the nurse who attended on Mr William.

Lucy pressed my hand. 'Tomorrow, dearest, tomorrow I will tell you all.'

She hurried from the room, and I sank into a chair by the fire, with my book lying open in my lap, unable to read a line, unable to think, except upon one subject – the secret which I was so soon to learn. If she had but spoken then! A few words more, and what unutterable misery might have been averted!

I was aroused from my reverie by Laurence, who came to challenge me to a game of billiards. On my pleading fatigue as an excuse for refusing, he seated himself on a stool at my feet, offering to read aloud to me.

'What shall it be, Bella? – *Paradise Lost*, De Quincey's *Essays*, Byron, Shelley, Tennyson –'

'Tennyson by all means! The dreary rain-blotted sky outside those windows, and the bleak moorland in the distance are perfectly Tennysonian. Read *Locksley Hall*.'

His deep melodious voice rolled out the swelling verse; but I heard the sound without its meaning. I could only think of the mystery which had been kept so long a secret from my lover. When he had finished the poem he threw aside his book, and sat looking earnestly at me.

'My solemn Bella,' he said, 'what on earth are you thinking about?'

The broad glare of the blaze from an enormous sea coal fire was full upon his handsome face. I tried to rouse myself, and, laying my hands upon his forehead, pushed back his curling chestnut hair. As I did so for the first time I perceived a cicatrice across his left temple – a deep gash, as if from the cut of a knife, but a wound of remote date.

'Why, Laurence,' I said, 'you tell me you were never thrown, and yet you have a scar here that looks like the evidence of some desperate fall. Did you get it in hunting?'

'No, my inquisitive Bella! No horse is to blame for that personal embellishment. I believe it was done when I was a child of two or three years old; but I have no positive recollection of the event, though I have a vague remembrance of wearing a sticking plaster bandage across my forehead, and being unconscionably petted by Lucy and my mother.'

'But it looks like a scar from a cut – from the cut of a knife.'

'I must have fallen upon some sharp instrument, – the edge of one of the stone steps, perhaps, or the metal scraper.'

'My poor Laurence, the blow might have killed you!'

He looked grave.

'Do you know, Bella,' he said, 'how difficult it is to dissociate the vague recollections of the actual events of out childhood from childish dreams that are scarcely more vague? Sometimes I have a strange fancy that I can remember getting this cut, and that it was caused by a knife thrown at me by another child.'

'Another child! What child?'

'A boy of my own age and size.'

'Was he your playfellow?'

'I can't tell; I can remember nothing but the circumstances of his throwing the knife at me, and the sensation of the hot blood streaming into my eyes and blinding me.'

'Can you remember where it occurred?'

'Yes, in the gallery upstairs.'

We lunched at two. After luncheon Laurence went to his own room to write some letters; Lady Adela and my aunt read and worked in the drawing room, while I sat at the piano, rambling through some sonatas of Beethoven.

We were occupied in this manner when Lucy came into the room, dressed for walking.

'I have ordered the carriage, mamma,' she said. 'I am going over to York to see that Beck has everything prepared. I shall be back to dinner.'

Lady Adela seemed to grow more helpless every day, – every day to rely more and more on her stepdaughter.

'You are sure to do all for the best, Lucy,' she said. 'Take plenty of wraps, for it is bitterly cold.'

'Shall I go with you, Lucy,' I asked.

'You! O, on no account, dear Isabel. What would Laurence say to me if I carried you off for a whole afternoon?'

She hurried from the room, and in two minutes the lumbering close carriage drove away from the portico. My motive in asking to accompany her was a selfish one: I thought it possible she might resume the morning's interrupted conversation during our drive.

If I had but gone with her!

It is so difficult to reconcile oneself to the irrevocable decrees of Providence; it is so difficult to bow the head in meek submission to the awful fiat; so difficult not to look back to the careless hours which preceded the falling of the blow, and calculate how it might have been averted.

The February twilight was closing in. My aunt and Lady Adela had fallen asleep by the fire. I stole softly out of the room to fetch a book which I had left upstairs. There was more light in the hall and on the staircase than in the drawing room; but the long gallery was growing dark, the dusky shadows gathering about the faded portraits of my lover's ancestry. I stopped at the top of the staircase, and looked for a moment towards the billiard room. The door was open, and I could see a light streaming from Laurence's little study. I went to my own room, contrived to find the book I wanted, and returned to the gallery. As I left my room I saw that the green baize door at the extreme end of the gallery was wide open.

An irresistible curiosity attracted me towards those mysterious apartments. As I drew nearer to the staircase I could plainly perceive the figure of a man standing at the half-glass door within. The light of a fire shining in the room behind him threw the outline of his head and figure into sharp relief. There was no possibility of mistaking that well-known form – the broad shoulders, the massive head, and clusters of curling hair. It was Laurence Wendale looking through the glass door of the invalid's apartments. He had penetrated those forbidden chambers, then. I thought immediately of the mystery connected with the invalid, and of Lucy's anxiety that it should be kept from her brother, and I hurried forward towards the baize door. As I advanced, he saw me, and rattled impatiently at the lock of the inner door. It was locked but the keys were on the outside. He did not speak, but rattled the lock incessantly, signifying by gesture of his head that I was to open the door. I turned the key, the door opened outwards, and I was nearly knocked down by the force with which he flung it back and dashed past me.

'Laurence!' I said, 'Laurence! What have you been doing here, and who locked you in?'

He did not answer me, but strode along the gallery, looking at each of the doors till he came to the only open one, that of the billiard room, which he entered.

I was wounded by his rude manner; but I scarcely thought of that, for I was on the threshold of the apartments occupied by the mysterious invalid, and I could not resist one hurried peep into the room behind the half-glass door.

It was a roomy apartment, very plainly furnished; a large fire burned in the grate, which was closely guarded by a very high brass fender, the highest I had ever seen. There was an easy chair close to this fender, and on the floor beside it a heap of old childish books, with glaring coloured prints, some of them torn to shreds. On the mantelpiece there was a painted wooden figure, held together by strings, such as children play with. Exactly opposite to where I stood there was another door, which was half-open, and through which I saw a bedroom, furnished with two iron bedsteads, placed side by side. There were no hangings either to these bedsteads or to the windows in the sitting room, and the latter were protected by iron bars. A horrible fear came over me. Mr William was perhaps a madman. The seclusion, the locked doors, the guarded fireplace and windows, the dreary curtainless beads, the watchfulness of Lucy, James Beck, and the nurse, – all pointed to this conclusion.

Tenantless as the room looked, the maniac might be lurking in the shadow. I turned to hurry back to the gallery, and found myself face to face with Mrs Peters, the nurse, with a small tea tray in her hands.

'My word, miss,' she said, 'how you did startle me, to be sure! What are you doing here? And why have you unlocked this door?'

'To let out Mr Laurence.'

'Mr Laurence!' she exclaimed, in a terrified voice.

'Yes; he was inside this door. Someone had locked him in, I suppose; and he told me to open it for him.'

'O miss, what have you done! What have you done! Today, above all things, when we've had such an awful time with him! What have you done!'

What had I done? I thought the woman must herself be half-distraught, so unaccountable was the agitation of her manner.

O merciful heaven, the laugh! The harsh, mocking, exulting, idiotic laugh! This time it rang out in loud and discordant peals to the very rafters of the house.

'O, for pity's sake,' I cried, clinging to the nurse, 'what is it, what is it?'

She threw me off, and rushing to the balustrades at the head of the staircase, called loudly, 'Andrew, Henry, bring lights!'

They came, the two men servants, – old men, who had served in that house for thirty or forty years, – they came with candles, and followed the nurse to the billiard room.

The door of the communication between that and Laurence Wendale's study was wide open, and on the threshold, with the light shining upon him from within the room, stood the double of my lover; the living, breathing image of my Laurence, the creature I had seen at the half-glass door, and had mistaken for Laurence himself. His face was distorted by a ghastly grin, and he was uttering some strange unintelligible sounds as we approached him, – guttural and unearthly murmurs horrible to hear. Even in that moment of bewilderment and terror I could see that the cambric about his right wrist was splashed with blood.

The nurse looked at him severely; he slunk away like a frightened child, and crept into a corner of the billiard room, where he stood grinning and mouthing at the bloodstains upon his wrist.

We rushed into the little study. O horror of horrors! The writing table was overturned; ink, papers, pens, all scattered and trampled on the floor; and in the midst of the confusion lay Laurence Wendale, the blood slowly ebbing away, with a dull gurgling sound, from a hideous gash in his throat.

A penknife, which belonged to Laurence's open desk, lay amongst the trampled papers, crimsoned to the hilt.

Laurence Wendale had been murdered by his idiot twin brother.

There was an inquest. I can recall at any hour, or at any moment, the whole agony of the scene. The dreary room, adjoining that in which the body lay; the dull February sky; the monotonous voice of the coroner and the medical men; and myself, or some wretched, shuddering, white-lipped creature that I could scarcely believe to be myself, giving evidence. Lady Adela was reproved for having kept her idiot son at Fernwood without the knowledge of the murdered man; but every effort was made to hush up the terrible story. William Wendale was tried at York, and transferred to the county lunatic asylum, there to be detained during Her Majesty's pleasure. His unhappy brother was quietly buried in the Wendale vault, the chief mausoleum in a damp moss-grown church close to the gates of Fernwood.

It is upwards of ten years since all this happened; but the horror of that February twilight is as fresh in my mind today as it was when I lay stricken – not senseless, but stupefied with anguish – on a sofa in the drawing room at Fernwood, listening to the wailing of the wretched mother and sister.

The misery of that time changed me at once from a young woman to an old one; not by any sudden blanching of my dark hair, but by the blotting out of every girlish feeling and of every womanly hope. This change in my own nature has drawn Lucy Wendale and me together with a link far stronger than any common sisterhood. Lady Adela died two years after the murder of her son. The Fernwood property has passed into the hands of the heir at law.

Lucy lives with me at the Isle of Wight. She is my protectress, my elder sister, without whom I should be lost; for I am but a helpless creature.

It was months after the quiet funeral in Fernwood church before Lucy spoke to me of the wretched being who had been the cause of so much misery.

'The idiocy of my unhappy brother,' she said, 'was caused by a fall from his nurse's arms, which resulted in fatal injury to the brain. The two children were infants at the time of the accident, and so much alike that we could only distinguish Laurence from William by the different colour of the ribbons with which the nurse tied the sleeves of the children's white frocks. My poor father suffered bitterly from his son's affliction; sometimes cherishing hope even in the face of the verdict which medical science pronounced upon the poor child's case, sometimes succumbing to utter despair. It was the intense misery which he himself endured that made him resolve on the course which ultimately led to so fatal a catastrophe. He determined on concealing William's affliction from his twin brother. At a very early age the idiot child was removed to the apartments in which he lived until the day of his brother's murder. James Beck and the nurse, both experienced in the treatment of mental affliction, were engaged to attend him; and indeed the strictest precaution seemed necessary, as, on the only occasion of the two children meeting, William evinced a determined animosity to his brother, and inflicted a blow with a knife the traces of which Laurence carried to his grave. The doctors attributed this violent hatred to some morbid feeling respecting the likeness between the two boys. William flew at his brother as some wild animal springs upon its reflection in a glass. With me, in his most violent fit, he was comparatively tractable; but the strictest surveillance was always necessary; and the fatal deed which the wretched, but irresponsible creature at last committed might never have been done but for the imprudent absence of James Beck and myself.'

NOTES

1. Gold-coloured alloy of copper, zinc and tin used in decorations.

2. Stream marking the boundary between Italy and Gaul, Julius Caesar crossed it in 49 BC thus committing himself to war. The expression has come to mean a point of no return.

3. Works whose descriptions of Switzerland moulded Victorian England's image of that country.

4. Tragic Byronic heroes who concealed dark secrets.

5. Manfred invoked the Witch of the Alps in order to grant himself relief from the tormenting sense of guilt he felt for an unnamed previous offence.

6. Alternative spelling of 'boulle', material used for inlaying furniture such as tortoiseshell or brass.

7. British government securities with fixed interest and without time limit.

8. 'Happen what may!'

Mary Elizabeth Braddon was born in London on 4th October 1835. Her father, Henry Braddon, separated from her mother, Fanny White, in 1839 and the young girl moved to St Leonard's-on-Sea in East Sussex with her mother.

Although she had been privately educated, in 1857 Braddon scandalously became an actress aged seventeen using the pseudonym Mary Seyton. In 1860, however, following a stint at The Royal Surrey Theatre in London, Braddon abandoned the stage to pursue a career as a novelist, having written *The Ocotroon: or the Lily of Louisiana.* She enjoyed some literary success that year, publishing her second novel and seeing her play, *The Loves of Arcadia*, performed at The Strand Theatre.

That same year she also met the periodical publisher John Maxwell, with whom she began a controversial relationship, despite the fact that he was still married to his institutionalised wife. Over the next few years, Braddon cared for Maxwell's five children and bore him six of her own, before marrying him in 1874, after the death of his first wife. It was for the inaugural edition of Maxwell's magazine, *Robin Goodfellow*, that Braddon was to write her most famous novel *Lady Audley's Secret* in 1862. There followed a prodigious number of novels, totalling more than eighty books.

She was an author of tremendous popularity and her books received great acclaim, her supporters including many famous names, amongst them William Thackeray and Henry James. Her novels, written for the working classes, were founding works in the genre of sensation fiction and often serve to expose the suppression of women and the hypocrisy of the upper classes, attacking self-satisfied morality and social pretensions. Braddon founded *Belgravia Magazine* in 1866 offering literature at affordable costs; in addition she founded *The Mistletoe Bough*, a Christmas Annual, in 1878.

Braddon died in February 1915 of a cerebral haemorrhage, following John Maxwell's death in 1895.

HESPERUS PRESS CLASSICS

Hesperus Press, as suggested by the Latin motto, is committed to bringing near what is far – far both in space and time. Works written by the greatest authors, and unjustly neglected or simply little known in the English-speaking world, are made accessible through new translations and a completely fresh editorial approach. Through these classic works, the reader is introduced to the greatest writers from all times and all cultures.

For more information on Hesperus Press, please visit our website: **www.hesperuspress.com**

ET REMOTISSIMA PROPE

SELECTED TITLES FROM HESPERUS PRESS

Author	Title	Foreword writer
Pietro Aretino	*The School of Whoredom*	Paul Bailey
Pietro Aretino	*The Secret Life of Nuns*	
Jane Austen	*Lesley Castle*	Zoë Heller
Jane Austen	*Love and Friendship*	Fay Weldon
Honoré de Balzac	*Colonel Chabert*	A.N. Wilson
Charles Baudelaire	*On Wine and Hashish*	Margaret Drabble
Giovanni Boccaccio	*Life of Dante*	A.N. Wilson
Charlotte Brontë	*The Spell*	
Emily Brontë	*Poems of Solitude*	Helen Dunmore
Mikhail Bulgakov	*Fatal Eggs*	Doris Lessing
Mikhail Bulgakov	*The Heart of a Dog*	A.S. Byatt
Giacomo Casanova	*The Duel*	Tim Parks
Miguel de Cervantes	*The Dialogue of the Dogs*	Ben Okri
Geoffrey Chaucer	*The Parliament of Birds*	
Anton Chekhov	*The Story of a Nobody*	Louis de Bernières
Anton Chekhov	*Three Years*	William Fiennes
Wilkie Collins	*The Frozen Deep*	
Joseph Conrad	*Heart of Darkness*	A.N. Wilson
Joseph Conrad	*The Return*	Colm Tóibín
Gabriele D'Annunzio	*The Book of the Virgins*	Tim Parks
Dante Alighieri	*The Divine Comedy: Inferno*	
Dante Alighieri	*New Life*	Louis de Bernières
Daniel Defoe	*The King of Pirates*	Peter Ackroyd
Marquis de Sade	*Incest*	Janet Street-Porter
Charles Dickens	*The Haunted House*	Peter Ackroyd
Charles Dickens	*A House to Let*	
Fyodor Dostoevsky	*The Double*	Jeremy Dyson
Fyodor Dostoevsky	*Poor People*	Charlotte Hobson
Alexandre Dumas	*One Thousand and One Ghosts*	

George Eliot	*Amos Barton*	Matthew Sweet
Henry Fielding	*Jonathan Wild the Great*	Peter Ackroyd
F. Scott Fitzgerald	*The Popular Girl*	Helen Dunmore
Gustave Flaubert	*Memoirs of a Madman*	Germaine Greer
Ugo Foscolo	*Last Letters of Jacopo Ortis*	Valerio Massimo Manfredi
Elizabeth Gaskell	*Lois the Witch*	Jenny Uglow
Théophile Gautier	*The Jinx*	Gilbert Adair
André Gide	*Theseus*	
Johann Wolfgang von Goethe	*The Man of Fifty*	A.S. Byatt
Nikolai Gogol	*The Squabble*	Patrick McCabe
E.T.A. Hoffmann	*Mademoiselle de Scudéri*	Gilbert Adair
Victor Hugo	*The Last Day of a Condemned Man*	Libby Purves
Joris-Karl Huysmans	*With the Flow*	Simon Callow
Henry James	*In the Cage*	Libby Purves
Franz Kafka	*Metamorphosis*	Martin Jarvis
Franz Kafka	*The Trial*	Zadie Smith
John Keats	*Fugitive Poems*	Andrew Motion
Heinrich von Kleist	*The Marquise of O–*	Andrew Miller
Mikhail Lermontov	*A Hero of Our Time*	Doris Lessing
Nikolai Leskov	*Lady Macbeth of Mtsensk*	Gilbert Adair
Carlo Levi	*Words are Stones*	Anita Desai
Xavier de Maistre	*A Journey Around my Room*	Alain de Botton
André Malraux	*The Way of the Kings*	Rachel Seiffert
Katherine Mansfield	*Prelude*	William Boyd
Edgar Lee Masters	*Spoon River Anthology*	Shena Mackay
Guy de Maupassant	*Butterball*	Germaine Greer
Prosper Mérimée	*Carmen*	Philip Pullman
Sir Thomas More	*The History of King Richard III*	Sister Wendy Beckett
Sándor Petőfi	*John the Valiant*	George Szirtes

Francis Petrarch	*My Secret Book*	Germaine Greer
Luigi Pirandello	*Loveless Love*	
Edgar Allan Poe	*Eureka*	Sir Patrick Moore
Alexander Pope	*The Rape of the Lock* and *A Key to the Lock*	Peter Ackroyd
Antoine-François Prévost	*Manon Lescaut*	Germaine Greer
Marcel Proust	*Pleasures and Days*	A.N. Wilson
Alexander Pushkin	*Dubrovsky*	Patrick Neate
Alexander Pushkin	*Ruslan and Lyudmila*	Colm Tóibín
François Rabelais	*Pantagruel*	Paul Bailey
François Rabelais	*Gargantua*	Paul Bailey
Christina Rossetti	*Commonplace*	Andrew Motion
George Sand	*The Devil's Pool*	Victoria Glendinning
Jean-Paul Sartre	*The Wall*	Justin Cartwright
Friedrich von Schiller	*The Ghost-seer*	Martin Jarvis
Mary Shelley	*Transformation*	
Percy Bysshe Shelley	*Zastrozzi*	Germaine Greer
Stendhal	*Memoirs of an Egotist*	Doris Lessing
Robert Louis Stevenson	*Dr Jekyll and Mr Hyde*	Helen Dunmore
Theodor Storm	*The Lake of the Bees*	Alan Sillitoe
Leo Tolstoy	*The Death of Ivan Ilych*	
Leo Tolstoy	*Hadji Murat*	Colm Tóibín
Ivan Turgenev	*Faust*	Simon Callow
Mark Twain	*The Diary of Adam and Eve*	John Updike
Mark Twain	*Tom Sawyer, Detective*	
Oscar Wilde	*The Portrait of Mr W.H.*	Peter Ackroyd
Virginia Woolf	*Carlyle's House and Other Sketches*	Doris Lessing
Virginia Woolf	*Monday or Tuesday*	Scarlett Thomas
Emile Zola	*For a Night of Love*	A.N. Wilson